# DEATH AT DEACON POND

Published by Lobster Press™
1620 Sherbrooke Street West, Suites C & D
Montréal, Québec   H3H 1C9
Tel. (514) 904-1100 • Fax (514) 904-1101 • www.lobsterpress.com

Publisher: Alison Fripp
Editors: Alison Fripp & Meghan Nolan
Editorial Assistant: Molly Armstrong
Cover Design: Jenn McIntyre
Graphic Design & Production: Tammy Desnoyers

We acknowledge the financial support of the Government of Canada through the Book Publishing Industry Development Program (BPIDP) for our publishing activities.

We acknowledge the support of the Canada Council for the Arts for our publishing program.

The Canada Council | Le Conseil des Arts
for the Arts | du Canada

Library and Archives Canada Cataloguing in Publication

Alexander, E. M., 1970-
        Death at Deacon Pond / E.M. Alexander.

ISBN-13: 978-1-897073-42-1
ISBN-10: 1-897073-42-9

        I. Title.

PZ7.A377De 2006                    813'.6                    C2006-900308-4

Printed and bound in Canada.

*For Phillip, who tells me "I can."*
*For Ethan, who reminds me "I must."*
*And for my brother Michael, whose face I still see everywhere.*

– E.M. Alexander

# DEATH AT DEACON POND

written by

## E.M. ALEXANDER

Lobster Press ™

# INTRODUCTION

**EVEN IN THE** faded light of day, he could see that the trip wire had been tampered with. Perhaps a curious animal had snapped the line; perhaps it was something more. His thoughts swirled, mingling with the light breeze around him. The plants in the field swayed their jagged leaves, giving off a soft rustle that had the sound of a secret whisper. Bending closer to the ground, he could see footprints. *Definitely an animal*, he thought, *but not the furry variety.*

He eyed the path made by the footprints and followed the clues they left behind. The prints stopped abruptly at the edge of a steep divide. Below, the terrain was uninviting, littered with sharp rocks. His keen eyes registered numerous dark stains. His head gave a small nod. The trap had done its job. There, crouched next to a boulder, lay a man who breathed so lightly he might already be mistaken for dead. He had not made it far.

"Help me," the man cried softly.

He didn't answer. Instead, he collected the discharged weapon. He located the casings and slipped them into his jacket pocket.

"Come on, man," the dying man gasped. "You can't leave me here to bleed to death."

He looked all the way down the steep ravine and he was struck by a feeling of vertigo – a flash he dismissed as quickly as it came. He turned back to the man and smiled. He held out his hand and began to pull the injured man to his feet. "Of course I wouldn't leave you here. We're partners." He felt the man sway weakly and cling to him like a forest vine. Briefly, they shuffled together. "Here," he said, gently. "Let me help you." He felt the man lean into him and loosen the grip on his hand. "That's it," he coaxed, "let me help you ... down." He shoved the injured man down the ravine with all his strength and watched his arms pinwheel as he tumbled out of sight.

It was time to call the crew. They would harvest early and then deal with the body. That way, he would not lose the whole crop, if the police were called. *It would have been simpler if that damned fool hadn't walked into the trap,* he thought. *Then again, that's just what he might be taken for – a damned fool that walked into his own trap and fell off a cliff trying to get help.*

He heard activity down at the beach and knew he had to work quickly. Before long, bonfire flames licked the blackening sky. Laughter wafted past the hazy smoke, parting the stillness of the night air. Concealed in the shadows, he lingered momentarily as an uninvited guest. When he had seen enough, he turned back silently, melting back into the shadows from which he had come.

# CHAPTER 1

**THE WARMTH OF** the fire eased over the front of Kerri's body, leaving her back exposed to the evening chill. Goose bumps prickled up her spine. A light breeze tossed her hair across her face. Between strands, she could see that the amber light of the flickering fire made her chestnut hair glow. Her cheeks began to sting, feeling hot and tight. *Time to flip*, she thought, and turned her back toward the flames. She shook her head and ran her fingers through her tangled hair in a feeble attempt to restyle it. As quickly as she raked her fingers through the fine, straight strands, the pieces would fall back out of place.

Couples paired off for privacy. Their secret sounds and low conversation made her edge closer to the fire. *Alone again*, she sighed. *How typical.* She took a sip of the beer she'd been holding and grimaced as the warm, bitter liquid slid down her throat. "Supposed to drink it while it's cold," she whispered to no one.

She chanced a look around. The night had transformed the beach at Deacon Pond into an unfamiliar place. She could not see the tiny waterfall that fed the pond with a continuous stream of water from the nearby rivers. The water was black with mystery, the sand shifting and unsure under her feet. The surrounding woods seemed to creep forward in the night, shrouding them all under its shadowy veil. Kerri wished she could simply leave, but even a short walk through the darkened woods was not an inviting prospect.

She felt a gentle nudge at her arm and knew at once that it was Seth. As he settled down on the log next to her, Kerri questioned why they always ended up alone together. Not that it ever mattered. Even when they were alone, they behaved as if they were surrounded by others. She wondered – not for the first time – why Seth had never made a move on her. She supposed it was because they had known each other all their lives. They had so much in common. *Maybe we just became such good friends because our fathers are both cops. Were cops,* she reprimanded herself. Three years later and she still made that mistake.

Still, Seth had always been there for her. After her father's funeral, their relationship seemed to be on the verge of moving to a deeper level. He had been freer with his affection, and he was always there when she needed a shoulder to cry on. But for some reason, they had never broken through the barrier of friendship. Kerri figured it was probably hard for him to see her as someone different when he had known her in pigtails and braces. Yet as she glanced at his profile, taking in the strong jaw and full lashes, she felt the familiar pull toward him. *He doesn't see me that way*, she told herself. *He never has. Becoming seniors in high school doesn't change that fact. Besides, I'm not his type – the cheerleader type.*

"I guess the party kind of broke up, huh?" he said, looking down as his sneakers busily dug small trenches to nowhere in the sand.

Kerri nodded but said nothing. She watched his feet working aimlessly. She waited for the jerky movements to stop. For a brief moment, she had to resist the urge to kick him. The old feelings were rising up within her, poisoning her mind. The twisted knot pulled tighter inside. Would it always be like this? Would she forever appear normal on the surface, but always fall short, like the disappointment of a desert mirage? *People see what they want to see*, she thought.

"Are you working at the store again this summer?"

"Yeah, that's what I planned on," Kerri answered. "I've got to bank every bit I can if I want to go to college next year. With my dad gone ..." She turned away, unable to finish.

Seth let the words linger in the air. He seemed unsure of how to respond. "Yeah, I think I'm going to end up at community college, if I'm lucky. It's all I can really afford."

Kerri turned to face him. She hated the flutter of hope she felt bursting in her chest. *If Seth went to community college, we could still hang out together. He might – oh, give it up! What's next? Are you going to enroll in all of his classes, so you can talk to him – just like you do now?*

"Yeah," she said, trying to sound normal. "It's all I can afford too."

He smiled. "You don't seem too excited. Community college is still college."

"I guess."

"My dad won't let me go away to school. I wanted to get out of this town, maybe go south where it's warm. A winter without snow sounded great, but now that my mom has left ..."

Kerri shot him a sideways glance. She wanted to ask if he'd heard from her, but the words remained trapped inside her throat. *His mom is another thing we can't talk about.*

"I'm going home. I'm beat," she said.

"I'll go with you. I doubt anyone will notice if we go." Seth gave a short laugh. Kerri knew he was right, yet her resentment grew within and burned like the fire before them. For once, she wanted to be the one who lost track of time. When would it be her turn to be the last to leave the party?

It was on the tip of her tongue to tell him not to bother leaving with her; that she was a big girl and could walk herself home. Yet, before the words left her lips, she knew she would accept his offer. "Give me a second. Nature calls, you know," she said with a giggle.

His laughter trailed after her as she walked into the periphery of the woods. She searched for a private spot and found one a bit deeper among the trees. The night noises buzzed around her head. Kerri settled into a secluded spot, careful to position her feet so that she would avoid her shoes. As she unzipped her jeans, she heard a twig snap behind her. "I'm not done, Seth," she said, irritably. There was no reply.

"Seth?" she whispered his name into the darkness. She whipped around, her breath coming in harsh gasps. "Seth, where are you? This isn't funny!" Kerri hurried, rushing back toward the beach. She hoped the panicky feeling would subside when she was near the warm firelight again, instead of surrounded by the thick blackness. As she crashed through brush, twigs cut across her arms, and leaves swatted at her face, but she pushed on without caring.

*I've got to get out of here. I've got to – oh shit,* she thought, her foot catching on a root. Toppling forward, she instinctively threw out her arms to break her fall.

*What the ... ?* She fell with an ungraceful thump. She reached out blindly, groping in an attempt to determine what had tripped her. Her fingernails raked across a stiff fabric. It made a ripping sound, like a cat scratching against a post. *Jeans,* she thought. Hysteria bubbled up. Her heart pounded in her chest. She felt a hard shin. Then her hand cupped a firm, muscular thigh. *This is no root.*

*Oh my God! I'm lying on a body!* Frantically, she scrambled to her feet. "Seth ... " she gasped, hoping it was him, hoping that he was playing a bad joke on her and that later they'd laugh about it. Then Kerri heard a low moan, followed by a softly whispered plea: "Help me." *That's not Seth. I'd know his voice anywhere and that's not it.*

Kerri's first thought was to run – to run fast and far from that voice – but her legs made no move. Her eyes betrayed her with only the vague outline of a man and a yellowy slant of teeth in a gaping mouth. "Hurt. Please, help me," the voice repeated, as Kerri felt her hand being clasped, gripped by a large, rough hand.

She tried to pull away. The touch was too invasive – too familiar. Like a fat worm working its way inside a piece of fruit, Kerri could feel an image trying to penetrate her mind. "Not now," she begged. She tried to fight against it, but the image was coming on fast and strong.

Suddenly, the dark woods fell away, changing like a scene in a movie. She now caught a glimpse of a green field as it flashed before her eyes. Hands that were not hers reached down. Kerri saw them grab a wire and follow its path in a slow, continuous motion. *"No!"* Kerri tried to scream, "Don't touch that!" But it was too late.

Pain erupted in her back. Her mind was spiraling like the foreign arms she could feel trying to maintain balance, before the momentary sensation of weightlessness gave way and she was falling. Down the hillside she went, feeling her bones jarring and her body being battered as she plunged farther and farther. What was it she was seeing? Her head throbbed. "Not supposed to be there," she whispered, and gave herself over to the black oblivion.

# CHAPTER 2

**KERRI CLUTCHED THE** faded blanket tighter around her, but it was useless. The thin wool could not combat the bone-chilling cold. She snaked a hand out from under the blanket, passing her fingers across her forehead in a quick massage. It did nothing to alleviate the dull ache in her head, but at least it gave her something to do with her hands. Never mind that the pain that had settled behind her temples would bring her misery for days. *The bigger the vision, the bigger the headache*, she thought wryly. *What a wonderful gift! It keeps on giving and giving like the world's crappiest charity.*

Kerri edged closer to the dying fire, listening to the low conversations that the police were having around the body. *God, they sound like bees buzzing around a hive!* She felt a perverse giggle welling up at the comic image, and she had to bite her lower lip to quell the laughter. *Besides, she thought more soberly, you know what else sounds like bees? Flies, that's what. And let's face it, flies like ... well ... they like dead things.* She recoiled at the thought, effectively muting any trace of laughter.

Streaks of yellow plastic caution tape were draped like party streamers, marking off the scene. Kerri followed the tape with her eyes, noting how it forced the officers to walk carefully in order to avoid breaking it. A camera flash flickered. Gloved hands plucked items from around the body, filling clear bags, marking them for evidence. She passed a trembling hand across her forehead, blocking her view.

"Are you okay?"

Startled, Kerri twitched involuntarily. "Jesus, Seth! You scared me!"

"I'm sorry," he said, taking a seat next to her. He shook his head at the scene before them. "I can't believe this," Seth said, with a shaky voice. "I know this guy!"

Kerri sucked in a breath. "You know him? How?"

"From the Shop N' Save – "

"What? I've worked summers there for the last three years and I've never seen him."

"That's because he doesn't come into the store. I've delivered groceries to his house lots of times." Seth shook his head, dazed.

Kerri imagined the dead man, receiving his grocery delivery, tipping the driver, putting his food away like anyone else. "What was he like?" Her voice sounded hollow.

"Huh?" Seth returned, baffled. "How do I know? I only brought him his orders."

Kerri turned her head away. She took a slow, shuddering breath. She didn't want to burst out crying. She closed her eyes, pressing her fingers lightly in the corners of her eyelids. Her fingertips came back wet. She flicked the moisture away, but it only smeared across her finger as if her skin were some impenetrable barrier. Around her, things moved slowly, almost as if she were dreaming.

Seth cleared his throat, startling her back into focus. "I thought he hurt you. You started to come around when the paramedics arrived. They said you fainted and that it was a good thing that you landed on ... "

"Stop right there," she said, warding off his words with a raised hand. His words crawled over her like hairy black spiders. Waking up on a corpse was right out of a horror movie. "What's his name?"

"Mark Travers. He lives back there." Seth pointed toward the woods, to an area beyond her range of vision. "I've heard things about him."

"Like what?"

Seth shrugged. "People say that the guy was a real nut job, had delusions or something."

The words knocked the wind out of her like a swift punch to the chest. "What do you mean?"

A pink tinge crept onto Seth's cheeks. "Um, I don't know," he stammered, turning his eyes toward the ground. "I just heard the guy is real paranoid, like he thinks the government is out to get him or something. I don't think he ever leaves his house."

"Oh." Kerri answered, wishing the earth would open

up wide and swallow her. *What would Seth think of me if he knew? Would he think I'm just another delusional psycho, a "nut job" in training?*

They fell back into silence, watching the police do their work. The old Victorian house Seth was referring to was perched high upon a hilly peak, overlooking Deacon Pond. She had heard someone lived there, but the house had always appeared secluded and dark. *It won't be like that much longer*, she thought. *The police will find their way there soon enough. They'll light up that house like a Christmas tree.*

Kerri wished she couldn't see him, but the dead man was fully visible. Under the unnatural brilliance of the police equipment, his body was illuminated like a specimen under a microscope. The man almost looked as if he were simply lounging at the foot of the large oak tree, his upper torso resting against the sturdy trunk.

It was his eyes that told her the truth. Open and unblinking, those blank eyes would never again do anything but stare vacantly. Kerri shuddered as she remembered the touch of his hand, the way he had shared his torment with her. She turned her head away, wishing she'd stayed home that night, wishing she could reverse time and put herself somewhere else. Anywhere would be better.

Not that it was the first time that she'd seen a dead man. She only wished that it was. She squeezed her eyes shut, willing the pain away. It was no good thinking about her father now. That seemed like a lifetime ago.

Yet, as much as she did not want to see what lay before her, Kerri could not stop herself from watching the dead man. Even though each glance brought the painful past fresh and new to the surface, Kerri's eyes kept traveling back to the dead man's face. Why did it feel as if she were reliving the worst day of her life? *It's not Dad*, she reminded herself. Kerri stared long and hard, until her eyes lost focus and the present faded away into an anonymous blur.

"I've got something over here!" Sheriff O'Connell shouted, his voice dragging Kerri out of her reverie. She could see him squatting low to the ground, his large frame still visible over the rock he was examining. "Henry, make sure you swab this blood." Maintaining his position, he called out to Officer Roberts. "Dylan, I think we have drag marks here. We're going to have to expand the scene."

Kerri watched as Officer Roberts, Seth's father, moved toward Sheriff O'Connell. She had known Officer Roberts for as long as she could remember. As her father's patrol partner, he and her dad had grown close. Over the years, they had taken turns cooking at numerous backyard barbeques and had spent the majority of their Friday nights together playing poker with friends. As he conferred with the sheriff, Kerri realized that she had not seen Dylan in a while.

*He used to come around all the time*, Kerri thought. *When Dad first died, he'd check on us every week. He said it was a cop thing; that the boys in blue knew how to take care of their own.* Cindy, Seth's mom, used to accompany him on the visits. Kerri's mom would shoo Cindy out of the kitchen if she tried so much as to stir the pasta sauce. Kerri almost smiled remembering that. She missed those visits. It had felt like family, even without Dad.

*How long has it been*, she thought, *since Dylan visited?* To Kerri, it seemed as though his visits to the Langston house had become less frequent, finally stopping altogether after Cindy had moved out six months earlier.

The split was still a touchy subject with Seth. As Kerri studied Officer Roberts, she noticed that his face was marked by harsh lines and a stern countenance, neither of which detracted from his rugged good looks. *The breakup must have been hard on him. Even so, Roberts is a veritable Marlboro Man*, Kerri reminded herself. *He's hardly one to wear his heart on his sleeve. Like father, like son.*

He bent to examine the marks Sheriff O'Connell had brought to his attention. "The guy was probably crawling for help," he offered.

"Maybe. Then again, maybe not. Grab Driscoll – you'll need an extra hand if we are going to preserve all the evidence." Roberts nodded. As he stood up, his eyes met Kerri's. He paused, then turned back to Sheriff O'Connell. Although they had lowered their voices to keep their conversation private, Kerri knew they were debating how to deal with her.

As Sheriff O'Connell began to walk toward her, his eyebrows knitted together in heavy concentration. Kerri wondered if O'Connell was weighing the benefits of taking her statement now or allowing her to go to the station house in the morning with her mother. After all, as her father had pointed out time and time again, the longer an individual waits to give an account of an incident, the less accurate that statement is likely to be.

Kerri reminded herself to stick to the facts. *What you saw might not be real*, she reprimanded herself silently. Dad always said that the first rule in police work is to follow the facts. You need hard evidence to prove what happened. Yet, as hard as she tried to think like an officer, Kerri knew she couldn't forget what she had seen. The dead man had shared something horrible with her, something that might be vital in revealing how he had died. Didn't she have a duty to make sure that this information came out?

She used to think so, but now she knew better. After his death, her father had shared something with her too. She had touched his cold hand, and he had shown her a piece of the day he died. There had been clues, but those clues had been tricks, lies that laughed at her. It had run through her head many times, each time revealing less.

*What I saw sure didn't help bring out the truth for Dad*, Kerri told herself. *This time, I will keep what I've seen to myself – at least until I figure out what my visions are trying to tell me.*

Was it that simple? After all, if she didn't want to know the truth, how could she rely on herself to reveal what had happened?

O'Connell was coming toward her. She could not look at him. She stared at his feet clad in black, shiny leather shoes that crunched on the gravel path with each step he took. For a moment, the woods and the dead man fell away, and she was a girl again, a younger girl in a busy police office with sweaty palms. She heard herself talking, looking down at a pair of black shoes and saying, "My father showed me. He showed me he didn't hurt himself."

And he had, right? Kerri had not understood at the time, but she had not forgotten what her father had told her.

"Kerri," her father had said when he was alive, "our eyes reveal the truth, if we can only bring our hearts to believe what they see."

Kerri opened her eyes. She was still in the woods. There was a dead body on the ground in the distance and a police officer moving in her direction. *Dad told me that what I see is the truth, or some version of the truth. He told me to believe in what I see.*

Kerri knew that she wasn't the girl she used to be. She could not hide under her bed any longer. She could not close her eyes and try to make it all disappear. She had seen something with her eyes, and now she would have to see it with her heart.

# CHAPTER 3

**AS SHERIFF O'CONNELL** appeared in front of her, Kerri wondered if he was mentally practicing how to deal with her. He had taken a statement from her before. Kerri doubted that the sheriff had forgotten when she had mistakenly told him about a vision. She had been so certain about what she had seen. Yet, looking back now, she wondered if she would have believed it herself. After all, she had just lost her father, and it was natural for her to find ways to deny his death. At least that was what everyone told her at the time.

*I was young and stupid then*, Kerri thought. *I'm not about to make the same mistake now.*

"Kerri," O'Connell began, "I am sorry you had to see all this." He indicated the scene with a wave of his arm. "You know, everyone still remembers your dad. He has been greatly missed around here."

Kerri nodded her head, not trusting her voice to

conceal the growing knot in her throat. He seemed sincere, but how much of the past did he remember? Would he handle her gently, concerned she might crack? *Maybe there's a great big "F" on my forehead – "F" for fragile? Fruitcake? Failure?*

"Listen, we're going to have to get your statement. Now is better, but considering the hell you've been through tonight ... well frankly, I think you should see a doctor to make sure you're okay."

"I'm fine," Kerri said. She met his eyes, trying to convey a sense of fortitude that she did not feel. Somehow, under the sheriff's penetrating gaze, she managed not to burst into tears. *I will not cry in front of him again. No way.*

"I understand from Seth that about a dozen kids were gathered here tonight?" When Kerri nodded, he continued. "Why don't you tell me the first thing you saw or heard when you went into the brush?"

"Well, it was pretty dark," she began hesitantly. "I thought I heard someone moving towards me, but I assumed it was Seth trying to freak me out. You know, shake me up so I'd be jumping at every little thing on the way home, and he'd have a good laugh."

"What happened next?"

"I wanted to get out fast, so I turned to run. That's when I tripped and fell on ... that's when I heard someone ask for help."

Kerri faced O'Connell, forgetting their past for a moment and thinking instead of her failure to help someone in need. She had failed because she had been afraid. She had thought only of her own safety, her own need to be disentangled from that part of herself that she could not control. That part of her that was all dark mystery, an unsolved puzzle with pieces that never fit together the right way. It made her different and kept her from trusting or getting too close to people.

"You heard the victim ask for help?" O'Connell questioned, looking up from his pad and pen. His voice penetrated like a blade.

"Yes, and my only instinct was to run. I should have been thinking about how I could help him, but I wanted to run. I wanted to get as far away as I could." As she said this, Kerri was flooded with shame. Her face burned and her shoulders lowered. She might have been able to help this man. Would he have lived if she had been calm instead of a scared little girl?

"According to Seth, he found you lying partially across the victim. Do you remember anything else?"

"No. I guess I passed out." *Keep it simple. Talk too much and you give yourself away, make yourself seem guilty.*

*I am guilty,* her inner self whispered. *I'm not telling him everything.*

*That's because I can't,* Kerri countered. *I don't know what's real.* She forced herself to look directly at the sheriff. She knew that credible witnesses were ones that gave the appearance of having nothing to hide – even if they had everything to hide. *A person with no secrets can always meet another eye to eye.*

Sheriff O'Connell hesitated, then asked, "Are you *sure* you heard the victim ask for help?"

Kerri's stomach tightened. She had said something wrong. *I heard him speak, right? Should I say that I'm not sure? That I hit my head?* Suddenly, the trip to the hospital had appeal.

"Yes," she said, slowly. "I'm pretty sure he said 'Help.' Why?"

The sheriff let out a small breath. "Well, it's simply impossible that he spoke to you, Kerri."

"Why? What do you mean?" But the truth was already beginning to dawn on her. She knew what he was going to say, what the coroner must have told him.

"Kerri, the preliminary findings suggest that the victim has been dead at least six hours. There is no way he could have spoken to you." He paused, his face softening. "Listen, Kerri, what you saw tonight would shake anyone up."

Kerri nodded, saying nothing. She was vaguely aware that her mouth hung open. It closed slowly. Sure, she was shaken up. Seeing a dead body would do that to anyone. A shiver ran down her spine, but she hardly moved. She felt stiff and unyielding, almost as if she were the corpse lying a few feet away. *Had Mark been dead all along? Did she have a conversation with a ghost?* Revulsion rose within her, but Kerri held it in check under O'Connell's watchful eye. The last thing she wanted was to give him a reason to think she knew more than she was saying.

*Besides, he wants to believe that I'm in shock, that I imagined the man ask for help. Let him think that if he wants to,* she thought. *I know the truth. I know what I saw, and I know what I heard.*

But did she? Could she trust what she had seen? Could she trust whatever power lived inside her that provided unwelcome glimpses into the minds of others?

Kerri tried to latch on to her faith before it fell away as fast as a landslide. Yet in her heart, she felt just like that awkward fourteen-year-old girl who once sat at Officer O'Connell's desk, trying to prove her father had been murdered. No one had taken her seriously then, and they certainly wouldn't do so now. Furthermore, how could she expect to be believed when she could not be sure of what she had seen? *It always comes down to proof,* she thought grimly, *and proof is what I need.*

# CHAPTER 4

**THE MORNING SUN** had begun to rise by the time he slipped soundlessly through the old, wooden door. A damp, earthy smell, fouled with the stench of sweat, urine, and rot, hit him.

He reached out, blindly tugging on the thin string he knew was there. The light of a single, bare bulb spilled into the room, quieting the muffled sounds of crying. *How much longer*, he thought, *before they realize their tears are useless?*

He prodded the unmoving body at his feet. She lay still to the touch, making no attempt to rise, or even open her eyes.

"Wake up," he snarled.

She gave no indication that she'd heard him. It was her body that looked different. No longer stiff and resistant, she graced the hard, damp floor like a battered carpet.

He had a moment of doubt. She had given him such trouble during the move. *Did I over-sedate her?* He put a finger to her neck. Her pulse throbbed steadily.

*Bitches*, he thought. *Fakes. Always up to some trick. You can't put anything past them.*

He felt a surge of hate rising up hot and fast, coursing through his veins. She'd been struggling again, he could see that. Her wrists were red and raw. Her clothes were twisted and disheveled, spotted with fresh dirt stains. And her face ... her face was weary and used-up – a pasty lump of uncooked dough.

*It's only been a week. They so quickly forget how to be human.* He gave a sharp kick to her stomach. "I said, wake up."

She moaned, opening her mouth enough for him to see how saturated her gag had become. She twisted her hands against the ropes, and her wrists began to bleed again.

He shook his head in revulsion. He'd take care of her first. It wouldn't do for her to rile up the others again. *She's too old, got too much fight in her.*

He bent down, brushing her hair from her face. "Too bad our time together is so short, darling. If we had longer, I think we'd have ourselves some fun, don't you?"

Her eyes opened at that point, as she tried to shrink away. She kicked at the air with her bound legs, her feet struggling uselessly. Her eyes pleaded with him, and he had to resist another urge to kick her. *Pathetic*, he thought. *What a waste. She looks like a helpless turtle on its back in the middle of the road.*

The image made him smile, and he reached into his pocket and primed the syringe.

# CHAPTER 5

**IT WAS THE** pain that awoke her. It was impossibly strong, and Kerri wondered how it could be attached to her body. Gingerly, she opened an eye, testing how hard it would be to face the day. She winced in reaction to the sunlight streaming into her bedroom. It was going to take more than two ibuprofens to knock her headache down.

Kerri staggered from her bed to the bathroom to raid the medicine cabinet. She tried to be as quiet as possible. Despite her efforts, the pills knocked against each other like beads in a rain stick. The brown pills looked pathetically small and useless in the palm of her hand. *Bottoms up*, Kerri thought, popping them into her mouth and grimacing as she swallowed them without liquid.

She checked the mirror, smiling wryly at the mess reflected back. She was going to need a long shower and about two days of sleep, neither of which she would have the luxury of today. She had to give a formal statement to the police this morning, and she had to do it in front of her mother.

*God, Mom hasn't been inside the police station since Dad died. Not even to clear out his desk and locker.*

Kerri remembered her mother crying for a week when Officer Roberts had finally delivered the boxed contents of her father's personal effects to them. She had never unpacked the box. In truth, Kerri didn't think her mother had ever even opened it. Instead, she had put it on the garage storage racks, as if opening it were akin to Pandora opening her box and unleashing all manner of disease and suffering upon the world. Kerri wondered if her mother thought that as long as the box remained closed, they were safe from further heartache. *It would have worked for Pandora, right?*

*But,* Kerri thought, *after all the bad stuff was released, the one good thing left in Pandora's box was hope. Too bad the girl had to wade through hell to get to it though.*

"Mom might be right," Kerri whispered. "I'm not exactly dying to find out what's inside Dad's box." Kerri splashed cool water on her face, rubbing the sleep from her bleary eyes. She could hear her mother's movements downstairs and could smell the rich aroma of coffee being brewed. *She's going to want me to eat breakfast.* Kerri groaned at the thought.

According to Lisa Langston, food was a necessary accompaniment to any situation. If you felt ill, it was time for orange juice and chicken soup. If you were celebrating, dessert was a must. Most importantly, if you had a difficult day ahead, breakfast would do the trick.

As she walked into the kitchen, her mother peered over at her from behind the morning paper. She hastily refolded the paper and tossed it to the far corner of the countertop. Kerri murmured, "Good morning." Aware she was under close scrutiny, she made a beeline for the coffee mugs.

"You look like you need to go back to sleep, Kerri."

"Mom, you know I have to go down to the station today." Kerri's fingers rubbed along her brow line, tracing the pain still shooting across her forehead.

"Headache?"

Kerri nodded. *No sense denying it.*

"Listen, I know you said last night that you were okay, but I made an appointment with Dr. Porter – "

"What? I don't need – "

"Kerri, I've made up my mind. Dr. Porter knows you so well." She grabbed a cloth and began to wipe imaginary crumbs off the countertop. "When I told him what happened last night, he insisted on seeing you."

"You mean *you* insisted," Kerri said. "I don't want to go. You know I don't want to take those pills anymore."

"Who said anything about medication? We just don't want you to have a setback. I've also called your boss, and he won't expect you at work for a while. Dr. Porter thought it would be best, just for a little bit, Kerri." She paused, softening her tone. "Last night must have been awful. I wish you hadn't seen ... " She broke off, seeming to have lost her voice. Kerri watched as she reassembled a composed face, adding, "You'll need a proper breakfast. No argument. We can't have you fainting dead away from malnutrition." Kerri sat mutely as she watched her mother spring into action. "Waffles or pancakes?"

"Pancakes would be great." Anything she ate would help place her mother's mind at ease. As she watched her mother bustling around the kitchen, at home in the task of preparing nourishment, Kerri hesitantly stated, "Mom, if you don't want to go with me today, I'll understand. I'll be fine."

Her mother's hands stopped working for a beat, before proceeding to crack delicate eggs and stir the thick batter. "Of course I'm going with you, Kerri," she said, quietly. "I'm going to put some fresh blueberries in these, won't that be nice?" Kerri watched her mother's mouth widen and lengthen into a smile. That smile was fixed upon her face, stiff and unbending like plastic.

Kerri's throat constricted. How was she going to swallow one blueberry, never mind a massive, doughy pancake? She offered her mother a quick grin. "Sure, Mom, blueberries sound great."

# CHAPTER 6

**AS THEY GOT** in the car to drive to the police station, Kerri concentrated on settling the unrest that was going on in her stomach. She had done her best to pick respectably at her breakfast and now regretted every bite she had taken. She swallowed hard, hating the juicy-feeling saliva in her mouth, hoping the food would stay down.

"I talked to Ann this morning," her mother said quietly.

Kerri's eyebrows shot up in surprise. "Did you tell her everything?"

The ignition roared to life. "We can't keep something like this from your sister, Kerri. I let her know we could handle this by ourselves." Her mother let out a pent-up breath. "I hate what the past few years have done to her. She used to be happy."

*We all were,* Kerri thought in silence, while out loud she murmured in quiet agreement. At twenty-one, Ann seemed to be a ghost of her former self. She had all but abandoned her college goals, except for half-hearted attempts at night classes that never seemed to get her much closer to a degree. She had drifted into a waitress job at the local diner and took classes only when inspiration and her bank account allowed.

Ann and their mother had fought constantly over Ann's life choices, finally driving Ann to move out. To Kerri, the arguments over the pointlessness of a job slinging coffee were simply a cover. Ann would never accept that their father's death was unresolved. *I didn't make it any better*, Kerri thought.

She looked out the window during the short drive into town, letting her eyes go out of focus, allowing each tree to blur into the next. Soon the trees were replaced by a smattering of small businesses, most of which resided in quaint, old-fashioned buildings – historic homes that had been remodeled. Kerri blinked hard, returning the world into view. They were almost there. *I hope I'm ready for this.*

The police station, like most things in Westford, was located on the main strip in town. Though it was unlikely the old brick building had seen a repairman in years, it still stood tall and regal like most turn-of-the-century buildings. The town prided itself on maintaining a historic image, even going way over budget during the enlargement of the town library in order to preserve its historical integrity. Kerri remembered that it was only last year that local citizens had protested remodeling the town green as well as a large department store chain that was interested in building on the outskirts of town. High school kids hanging out at Romanelli's Pizza Palace on a Saturday night often laughed at the display of old pictures that showed what the downtown area used to look like. But Kerri thought that other than adding pavement and better stores, the town had basically stayed the same for the past century.

"Are you ready?" Kerri's mom asked.

"As I'll ever be," Kerri returned, the words catching in her throat. The blue, cloud-dusted sky disappeared under the high, arched doorway, which was lined with granite blocks that were eerily reminiscent of teeth. As she walked into the building, Kerri could not escape the feeling that she was being swallowed alive by a giant, yawning mouth.

Inside, the office was alive with jangling phone lines and rustling papers. Coffee was dispensed liberally in Styrofoam cups, toted from one work station to another. Her mother approached the front desk to announce their presence, and Kerri's gaze lingered on her, noting that her mother's eyes darted everywhere with no desire to register anything they saw. *This is going to be tough*, Kerri thought.

"Well, they know we're here." Her mother tried to keep her voice bright, but to Kerri it sounded shaky and unsure.

"It's all right, Mom." Kerri gave her mother's cold hand a quick squeeze. "I'm okay. Last night ... well, it was awful ... but that doesn't mean that today has to be like – like last time." She paused, unsure if she should say more. Her mother's face was in danger of crumbling, as if one small pebble would be the difference between maintaining the status quo and causing major commotion. Kerri gave her hand another squeeze.

*No*, she thought, *it won't be like last time.* Kerri shuddered to recall how positive she had been that she had found the key to reopening the investigation into her father's death. She had been certain that what she had seen had been real. Back then, for the first time, Kerri had felt as though the visions that frequented her mind had a purpose of more than silly parlor tricks that helped to find lost toys or make lucky guesses on tests she hadn't studied for. She'd held something concrete, something that mattered. Something important that could make a difference.

So she had convinced her mother, who up until that point had always dismissed Kerri's visions as simply a young girl's active imagination. Her mother had believed what Kerri said because she desperately clung to any answer that countered the police report.

*I was a kid back then – too young and stupid. I had forgotten that police are ruled by the evidence they uncover. Police reports are filled with facts. If they have any doubt about a case, it heads for the circular file.*

She had read the pity on their faces. "Too emotional," they said; and that "it was a natural reaction" to want to disprove the conclusions that had been drawn, to deny the truth. Who would want to believe that their father had ended his own life? There it was in black and white – a cop found with a single shot to the head, fired from his own weapon, by his own hand. Without any other evidence, John Langston's death had been ruled a suicide.

Suicide. It was that single word that had become hard to accept. That word drew conclusions about the Langston family's life, marking it as a failure. They might as well have said that the happiness the family had shared was false, and in essence, that their lives were false. At the time, her vision had given her hope. She had seen her father's hand reaching to something – something shiny, bright – a star? His familiar water-resistant watch, the one with the brown, braided strap that Kerri had given him as a gift for Father's Day, had caught on something, falling into the dust. Kerri had heard the resounding shot and the collapse of his body. It had sickened her to hear that.

Yet her mind would not let her see her father lying vulnerable on the ground. Instead, it kept bringing her back to the watch and its broken clasp in the dirt. Over and over she watched as a gloved hand reached down to pick up the watch, realign the broken pin, and refasten the strap. The gloved hands had worked quickly, returning the watch to her father's wrist.

No one could understand the pain of seeing her father's death through his eyes. She had felt helpless reliving the worst moment of her life – and his – again and again, never able to change a thing or piece together the whole picture.

No matter how many times the scene replayed in her head, the images only became more distant, making Kerri feel as if she was chasing a ghost, trying to grab it in her hands as if that were possible, as if a ghost could ever be flesh and blood. At her mother's insistence, the watch had been dusted for prints. Nothing had been found, save for a minute amount of powder residue, consistent with common brands of latex gloves. Kerri had since wondered how a man could die on a crystal clear day, under blue skies and brilliant sunlight. Her sight had failed to answer that question.

Since then, Kerri had been careful. She did not talk to her mother about anything she saw that was not tangible. What her mind showed her was not reliable. Her mind told lies and half-truths. The story it told about her father had all but destroyed her family, giving them unfounded hope. *That won't be happening this time. Not if I can help it.*

# CHAPTER 7

**SEATED AT SHERIFF** O'Connell's large oak desk, Kerri told herself to keep it together. *We're in the homestretch now. O'Connell merely wants to formalize what we talked about last night. He hasn't even mentioned the part about the guy talking to me.*

Kerri glanced quickly at her mother, who stood stiff and pale. *Like a corpse,* Kerri thought involuntarily. She turned away, wishing she could banish these unbidden thoughts from her head. O'Connell didn't look much healthier. *By the looks of those dark circles around his bleary eyes, I'd say he hasn't slept yet. Yes, up all night. After all, he must have to answer to somebody.*

"Listen, Kerri, I know last night was stressful for you. I think I'm all set on your statement. I just need you to verify everything in it and sign it."

Kerri nodded in compliance, yet the deafening silence as she read the statement made it difficult to comprehend the words. As her mother leaned over her shoulder, Kerri's stomach clutched painfully around the leaden pancakes she had eaten.

"'Witness states she heard the victim call for help?'" Her mother's voice was high and panicky. "Kerri, was this man alive?"

Kerri's eyes danced to and fro between her mother and O'Connell. "I thought I heard something – " she said haltingly, "but I guess I was wrong." As her mother's face grew paler, Kerri's voice shrank down to a whisper. She welcomed O'Connell's quick intrusion.

"Mrs. Langston – Lisa – let's not get worked up here." He motioned downward with his hands. "Kerri was under a great deal of stress. Sometimes, in situations like this, a person might think they see or hear something that simply isn't there." He paused for a moment, lightening his tone. "You'd be surprised how often a witness is wrong."

Kerri watched her mother nod mutely. She could only guess what thoughts were racing through her mind. "I thought Seth was screwing with me, Mom. I got it wrong. That's all."

Kerri watched her mother's face working, clearly wanting to accept the logical explanation. "Do you have all you need then, Sheriff O'Connell? I am anxious to get Kerri to the doctor."

"We're about done. Why don't you help yourself to a cup of coffee? I would like a few minutes alone with Kerri."

Her mother jumped to her feet. "There is no way I'm going to – "

"Lisa," O'Connell interjected, "I know what you're thinking, but you are way off. I have to ask her questions regarding her friends. Now, you know as well as I do, I'll have a whole lot more success if you aren't here listening."

Despite the cold glare in her mother's eyes, Kerri surprised herself by saying, "It will be fine, Mom. Really." *Nothing could be further from the truth*, she thought. Her palms were slick with sweat. Her head made dull thumps that matched the quickened pounding of her heart. Although her mother retreated, her eyes remained fixed and wary.

O'Connell leaned forward, placing his elbows on the desk. He tapped his outstretched fingertips lightly against each other, before clasping them together. "Kerri, we have the autopsy report, and it confirms what we already suspected at the scene. This case is a homicide investigation."

"Murder?" Kerri whispered. Her icy fingers clasped her mouth. Her pulse raced. Had someone else been in the woods, watching them, waiting for them to find the body? *No*, she thought, *the wire in my vision was connected to something*. She turned her face away so O'Connell would not read the comprehension in her eyes. She saw Mark pull again at the wire and lose his balance. She wanted to cry out. Her jaw clamped tight. She clutched the arms of her chair, swallowing hard.

"I'm sorry, Kerri. I know this has got to be tough for

you," said O'Connell quietly.

His words were as disconnected and distant as a scene on television. Surely this must be happening to another girl, not her.

Sheriff O'Connell was speaking again. Kerri strained to focus on what he was saying. "The victim's name was Mark Travers, forty-two years old. He was five feet ten, medium build, brown hair, brown eyes. Our guys were able to ID him right away, since he has a prior record. His priors were ancient history, really. Small stuff like petty larceny and possession, but the guy did have a reputation. Most folks say he was a bit of a recluse. He had no family – parents died in a car wreck fifteen years ago. He inherited their place, up past Deacon Pond. I understand he used to fish there pretty regularly." He paused, watching her for signs of recognition. "Mr. Travers suffered numerous contusions from a fall, including a few broken bones, but the cause of death was determined to be a gunshot wound to the back."

Kerri chewed the soft inner tissue of her cheek to keep from making a sound. She recalled the pain in her back that she had experienced during last night's vision, and she had to resist an urge to rub the phantom wound. Mark's fall repeated, and she wished she could wash the image away – cleanse her head like a shower and let the unwanted thoughts simply slip down the drain into darkness.

"Kerri, I wondered if you could answer a few questions I have concerning Seth."

"Seth? What about Seth?"

"Well, are you aware that Seth knew the victim?"

"Sure, he was freaked out when he recognized him. He was a customer of his at the Shop N' Save."

"Seth has been a delivery guy for them for – how long – two, three years?"

"Yeah, that sounds about right. Ever since he could drive, I guess," she answered, but remained confused.

"Were there any drugs at the party last night?"

"No," said Kerri, indignant. "What's this all about?"

"I guess you haven't seen the morning paper." He shuffled through the papers on his desk, retrieving the latest edition of the *Daily Bulletin*. He pushed the paper across the desk toward her. "Last night, we found the remains of a large field of ditch weed – marijuana," he said with emphasis. "It was on the victim's property."

"Oh my God," whispered Kerri. "This guy was growing pot?"

O'Connell lifted his shoulders momentarily. "We can't be certain yet, but it gets worse. We also found what appears to be the remnant of a booby trap around the marijuana field. Even though we didn't find a gun of any kind on the scene, we think that it is possible Mark stumbled upon a trigger-loaded weapon."

"So Mark might have killed himself?" Kerri hated the sound of those words coming out of her mouth.

O'Connell shrugged. "It's possible, and if he did, someone knew about it because we didn't find a gun at the scene. Listen Kerri, we talked to everyone who was there last night. No one had any connection to Travers – except Seth."

Kerri nodded. "Yeah, Seth told me that last night. He said he used to deliver groceries to the guy, but I don't know if I'd call that a connection," she added.

O'Connell capped his pen and put it in his breast pocket. "We have to check out any lead, no matter how unlikely, and because Seth has had a prior conviction for possession ... "

"You can't believe ... No. That was a long time ago!" Kerri spat angrily. It was true that Seth had been in trouble before. Stressed and hurt over his mother's desertion, he had made a few stupid choices. *Things have changed though. He's not like that anymore,* she thought. *There is no way he'd be involved in anything like this.* "Listen, I know he got busted before, but that was stupid kid stuff. I know Seth. I hang out with him all the time."

O'Connell folded his arms across his chest and nodded slowly. "That may be true, but I can tell you one thing – I checked the delivery records from the Shop N' Save. There were no deliveries on record to Mark's home. What's more, I pulled Seth's employee file. Some of his customer log and tip tally sheets were missing. According to the manager, those records are supposed to be turned in at the end of every shift. Why would Seth say he delivered groceries to Mark, then sabotage his alibi?"

Kerri could only stare back blankly. *Why, indeed?*

# CHAPTER 8

**ANN WAS WAITING** for them when they got back home. Kerri was relieved to see Ann's car in the driveway. *I need to not be alone with Mom right now,* Kerri thought. *I don't know what to say to her, and I don't want to take a chance that I'll say the wrong thing.*

The return drive had been under a weighty silence that neither knew how to break. Kerri had spent the time trying to fill the gaping holes created by O'Connell's bombshells. Questions buzzed inside her aching head. *Why had Seth lied? Had he known about the pot? Was he using again?*

Ann had barely waited for the car to come to a stop in the driveway before her hand was opening Kerri's passenger-side door. "Are you okay? I wanted to be here sooner. I would have, if I'd known." She cast a stony look toward their mother, before examining Kerri with closer scrutiny. Ann had always been able to uncover more than

Kerri was willing to show. *Perhaps she has her own gift,* thought Kerri.

"I'm all right, Ann." Kerri waved her away, heading for the front door. "I'm not hurt or anything. It was just ... bad luck."

"Happens pretty often to us," Ann remarked dryly.

Kerri expected her mother to quiet Ann's pessimism, but instead she excused herself. "Girls, I think I'd better lie down. I didn't get much sleep last night." She climbed slowly up the stairs to her room without glancing back.

Kerri took a seat in the living room, while Ann fished two Excedrin out of her purse before disappearing into the kitchen. "You got any soda?" she called to Kerri.

"Yeah, why?"

Ann returned with a glass of Coke. "Because sometimes the caffeine can help the medicine work faster. Here, take these." She handed the pills and soda to Kerri. "You obviously have a whopper of a headache."

Kerri took the pills without denying it. She waited for Ann to let go of the restraint that held her tongue.

"Tell me what happened, Kerri. Everything." She crossed her arms with a firmness that suggested she expected a fight.

Once again, Kerri told the story. As she had with her mother, she stuck to the facts, relating the events as though they had happened to someone else. When she had finished, Kerri marveled at the unsatisfied look on her sister's face.

"Kerri, I know you too well. I know about your

headaches and what causes them. You might be able to fool Mom, but I'm not buying it. Tell me what you really saw."

Kerri turned away, unable to meet her sister's intense glare. Every time she saw something, it brought nothing but pain and problems. *I never see anything that is absolute. It is always grey, like murky water you don't want to step in.* She glanced back at Ann, thinking for the thousandth time that Ann could have handled this personality flaw far better than she ever had. *She always believes. She's been like that from the start,* Kerri thought. *Like when I saw Petey.*

Kerri had been five when Petey, their aging golden retriever, had died from a cancerous tumor. A week later, she'd seen him, running in their yard, happily playing with his favorite chewed-up Frisbee. She had run to the kitchen, shouting to her parents that it had all been a mistake. That Petey was fine. Her parents had not even looked out the window to see. Her mother had pulled her into her arms, her tongue making sympathetic clicking noises as she rocked Kerri back and forth. But Ann had gone outside. She had searched the yard, looking for any trace that suggested Petey had been there. Later, when they had gone to bed, Ann had crept into her room, slid beneath the covers with her and asked, "How did Petey look?"

*No one believed me,* Kerri thought, *no one but Ann.*

*But I've been down this road before.* Kerri let out a long sigh. Ann wouldn't be easy to fool. "Listen," Kerri began, "say I did see something ... say I saw something that, as usual, doesn't make any sense. So what? I can't prove it, so it doesn't mean anything."

Ann nodded and drew in a slow breath. She smoothed a steady hand over her shiny, brown hair. "You have good reason to think that way, but you can't let what you don't understand frighten you." She leaned in closer and placed her hand on Kerri's knee. "You have something. I don't understand it either. I only know that you can't pretend it doesn't exist."

Kerri attempted to swallow down the lump that was suddenly constricting her throat. *How can Ann still believe in me? How can she continue to have faith in something that Mom won't even acknowledge?*

Yet Ann had always had faith. No matter how often Kerri's mind gave false hope by applying easy lies, Ann had remained steady. *She deserves better than this*, Kerri thought. *I bet if it were Ann who had visions, instead of me, she'd have figured out how to use them. Ann would have kept at it. She would have forced the visions to come, until she knew how to make sense of them, until she figured out how to make them work for her.*

*And she wouldn't have wasted time, struggling against it or whining about how she wished she were a normal girl. Ann would have accepted her psychic powers for what they were and would have found a way to accept herself as well.*

Ann rose and gave Kerri's shoulder a gentle pat. "When you are ready to talk," she said, "I'll be ready to listen." With that, she walked quietly out of the house. Kerri heard the car engine fire up, followed by the crunch of gravel, grinding as Ann pulled away.

Only then did Kerri let the tears slip from her eyes. Her chest ached, and she let out a small, strangled cry. Sometimes Kerri wished that Ann didn't believe in her visions. Then they could pretend that everything was normal. They could forget that Kerri had once made them believe that she'd had proof that their father had not committed suicide. Visions could be misread. Visions could offer hope only to rip it away. Kerri had seen it happen with the vision of her father. She had seen how faith in her sight could be treacherous to the heart – especially to Ann's heart, which had always made her so quick to believe.

Ann hadn't said a harsh word when Kerri's vision had been wrong, but she didn't have to. The beaten look upon Ann's face had been worse than a blow to Kerri's gut. Kerri had promised right then and there that she would never make Ann suffer needlessly again. She would say nothing of her visions unless they could be proven with hard facts. Ann was the only one who believed. *If I squander away Ann's faith, where will that leave me, except all alone? No matter what,* she thought, *I cannot fail Ann again.*

# CHAPTER 9

**KERRI WAS DREAMING** of Petey. A nice dream. She was little again, and Petey could still make the most spectacular Frisbee catches. His powerful legs propelled him high in the air. His body did a half-twist before he ran back to her. She laughed, giving Petey a friendly scratch behind his ears. "Good boy," she said.

Then Kerri felt a tap at her shoulder. The smile dropped from her face, and the Frisbee slipped from her grasp. Mark Travers was there, his hand held out expectantly. "Can I have a turn?" he said.

Kerri awoke with a start as the shrill telephone ring pierced through the air. Uncurling her body from the couch, she grabbed the phone before it could disturb her mother. *Just a dream*, Kerri told herself, as she rubbed sleep away from her eyes. "Hello?" Kerri mumbled.

"Kerri? It's Beth," the girl on the other end blurted out in a rush. "What the hell happened last night? Are you all right? Mike talked to Seth this morning ... I can't believe this! I mean, me and Mike, well we were ... you know ... I didn't see a thing. I told the cops that – "

"I'm fine," Kerri said, breaking in. She smiled wryly, thinking that at last Beth had a real problem to panic over, rather than the dramas she invented to make life more interesting. "Last night was pretty awful, but I'm okay. How is Seth?" Kerri asked the question tentatively, surprising herself by how intently she was listening for the answer. Before last night, she had been confident that she knew Seth as well as she knew herself. Now she saw only a thick, unmoving fog between them.

"Oh my God, you haven't heard," Beth lowered her voice. "They asked Seth to take a drug test! He refused, but they can make him take one, because he's still on probation."

Kerri wished desperately that she had not answered the phone. Wondering if Seth had slipped up was far better than knowing for sure. "I have to go, Beth. I'd better talk to him myself."

"Are you going to be all right? Maybe I shouldn't have said anything ... "

"It's okay, don't worry about it. I'll talk to you later, all right?" Kerri placed the phone down, feeling her head pound anew. What was going on with Seth? He was never high around her, she knew that for sure.

*He's not around me all the time though. His dad works a whole lot of late nights, and with his mom gone ... there is opportunity, to say the least,* Kerri thought. Her hand hovered over the phone keypad, ready to punch in the familiar numbers, when the phone rang again. Kerri was startled and barely listened as Bob, her boss at the Shop N' Save, told her she could pick up her last paycheck on Friday.

"Last paycheck? What are you talking about?"

"Your mother told me you needed to take a leave of absence. I mean, that's fine and all, but I need a warm body in here now. I gave your hours to Stacy. I'm sorry, Kerri, but the store is too busy for me to be running it shorthanded." He had hung up before Kerri realized that he hadn't said good-bye.

"Who needs that stupid job anyway?" Kerri yelled into the receiver, but there was no answer, only the steady buzz of the dial tone as it droned in her ear.

*Um, I do*, she thought. *Last time I checked, college wasn't free. I don't know how much kindergarten teachers make, but Mom isn't exactly rolling in the dough.*

Kerri groaned out loud and flopped into a seat by the window. The house was quiet and warm from the early afternoon sun shining in through the blinds. She put the phone down and walked through the front door to the inviting warmth of the beautiful summer day. She was struck by how the clear, blue sky and brilliant radiance of the sun could be constant when last night had proved that life was anything but.

Kerri had no idea where she wanted to go, but she knew she wanted to go somewhere. Her feet moved, almost completely on their own volition. She knew she should leave a note, that her mother was likely to worry, but her need to get away from home was far too pressing.

She walked a few blocks until she reached the wooded area that served as her shortcut. There was a hole there, hollowed out of the brush, a perfect space between the trees that she could duck into. Quickly, she was swallowed up by the woods. *Like Alice, following the white rabbit into Wonderland,* she thought. *Except, of course, I've never run into any talking animals.*

As Kerri trekked through the familiar wooded path leading to Deacon Pond, she felt a sense of urgency she couldn't explain. Her feet moved faster, her heart began to race. She felt watched, despite her obvious solitude. It was as though the trees had grown eyes, and she had to fight an irrational need to look over her shoulder.

"Don't be ridiculous, Kerri," she said in a husky whisper. The leaves at her feet seemed to rustle in agreement. She continued on, moving briskly, easily avoiding all the tree roots and rocks that jutted out of the earth. The branches swayed in her wake, pulling wisps of hair from her neat ponytail. The familiar, earthy scent of decaying foliage blended with the new summer growth. The smell invaded her nostrils, making her nose run freely. She inhaled deeply, both relishing and hating the harsh burn she felt as air filled her lungs.

Kerri walked until her mind began to go blank. She didn't want to think anymore. *Go away Petey and go away Mark,* she thought.

*Sorry Dad, but you too. Please, just go away for now.*

Kerri could swear she felt a release. It was as though she'd been stuffed and now finally felt comfortable – like the year she ate three helpings on Thanksgiving and had to rip off her belt so her stomach could breathe. A weight tumbled off her now and she began to run faster. Her feet pounded the ground. She sailed over a rotten stump. Her legs were strong. They could take her anywhere. Nothing or nobody could stop her now.

She let go of every thought and worry in her head. She allowed the numbing feeling to overtake her in an oddly welcoming way. She pushed harder, until the thoughts in her head became elusive and she could no longer claim them as her own. By the time Kerri reached the beach, she was in a full run, panting hard.

# Chapter 10

**A SLOW, SNAKY** smile crawled upon his face as he saw her run past. Sheltered by the low brush, he had only to wait until her footsteps receded before slipping back out undetected.

At first, he worried that she would make things difficult, but seeing her run past him like an animal sensing the hunter's gun made him think differently. Her panic eased over him, and he wore it like a pair of comfortable old jeans.

*She's just a scared little girl, all alone in the woods,* he thought. *Let's hope she keeps out of my way.*

His face hardened. His lips flattened into a thin line. *She'd better.*

Things were moving too fast now. He could not afford to waste his time keeping track of a nosey little girl. But there were other ways he could make sure that she minded her own business.

*Yes*, he thought, smiling. His lips uncurled slowly, like the lazy movement of a cat's tail. *I know exactly who I can get to keep a close watch on her. The answer has been in front of me the whole time.*

He nodded, pleased with the plan. It was perfect. Soon, it would be time to leave this sleepy little town. With so many cops sniffing around, he couldn't take chances.

*It's time to move on*, he thought.

Leaving wouldn't be so bad. He had his contacts. It wouldn't take him long before he set up shop again. And who knows? Maybe in time he could come back. If he wanted to, that is. He'd keep his ear to the ground and wait. He could be patient.

But for now, it was time to get to work.

# CHAPTER 11

**KERRI REACHED THE** sandy beach and sat upon a faded rock to catch her breath. The hard surface had retained enough warmth from the sun to provide comfort. She watched the still water, listening to the easy quiet of birds calling to one another. Her eyes stared long enough to go out of focus. Still, Kerri could not keep from thinking about Seth. *Why would he lie to me? Why couldn't he come clean about what was going on?*

Kerri didn't know who to believe, but she could not ignore the possibility that Seth might be smoking pot again, that he might be more involved with Mark than he'd claimed. She tried to shrug off the heavy thoughts, preferring to enjoy the solitary serenity of the landscape that surrounded her.

As she looked across the pond, her eye caught on a spot of blue that was out of place in the middle of the dark water. Kerri thought it was an old rag, yet it was larger and had some form to it. She stood up and blinked her eyes hard to regain focus. The rag began to change. The object increased in size and shape until she recognized that what she saw was a still, floating body.

*That face*, Kerri thought. *Oh my God, I know that face!* It was a face that was emblazoned in her mind. A face she wouldn't forget for a long time. There, in front of her, was the man she had touched last night – the dead guy, Mark Travers. Kerri opened her mouth to scream. A ragged breath escaped her lips as she stepped back, wanting to erase the sight, wanting to escape. Suddenly, the dead man's eyes were no longer vacant. Those dark, watery eyes were alive.

Although his lips were moving, Kerri could only hear the sharp ache of her breathing, which was a rushing sound in her ears. She could feel a scream welling up in her throat, growing larger, but before she could open her mouth, the image vanished as suddenly as it had appeared. Kerri could see nothing but the sun as it glinted off the sparkling water. "But I saw it," she whispered aloud. "I know I saw it." She had seen Mark, as sure as she had seen Petey, playing in their yard so long ago.

*But this is different, right? When I saw Petey, he'd been dragging around that old Frisbee, something I'd seen him do about a million times. But the dead guy – Mark – he was in the woods. He did not drown in the pond. And besides, when I touched him, he was already dead.*

*Touched*, she thought. *I touched them. Maybe that's all it takes. Does that mean that anyone, anything, I touch could end up haunting me in some way?* Kerri thought of her father just then. Why did she only see his death, over and over, as if she were trapped inside his body? Why did she see Petey after his death, as if he were alive?

Kerri didn't know. Maybe it was because things had been different with Petey. Petey had been old. When he had died, it had simply been his time.

*No,* she thought. *That wouldn't explain Mark. He wasn't sick or old. He was young and he died violently, all alone. Yet, I see him differently every time, too – just like Petey.*

With Petey, Kerri got the feeling that it was just a visit, similar to the way a live dog would run up for a friendly pat on the head. *I think that it's Petey's way of showing me that he's all right. With Mark, I feel as if he's trying to show me something too. Only maybe he already has, and I just don't know what it is.*

Then there was her father. Kerri knew her father would not put her through so much pain if he wasn't trying to tell her something. Yet what he wanted to communicate to her always became garbled somehow. Each time she had the vision of her father it was as if she was in the Gallery Theater for the "Midnight Monster Movies" that ran on Saturday night. At first, the old monster films would roll fine, but at a crucial moment they would cut out. Dracula froze just as he was about to sink his pointy teeth into his victim. The screen would flicker because the reel was either broken or worn thin by overuse. Kerri's vision of her father was the same. It was as if the film could be spliced together, but it was always in danger of snapping before Dracula could strike, before her father could show her what she needed to see. *How can I get my visions of Dad to move forward? What am I missing?* Kerri tried to ease the pounding in her heart as she scanned the water for the body. Her legs felt wet, and she realized that she was standing knee-deep in the warm, bronze-colored water. Her sneakers oozed as she paced the shoreline. With her hand cupped over her eyes, Kerri climbed up onto a large boulder, but the higher vantage point offered no clues. Defeated, she sat on the shore. *I'm going crazy,* she thought. She gave a shaky little laugh, thinking how fortunate it was that her mother was not witnessing this scene. Kerri knew that it would be all the fuel her mother would need to validate a visit to Dr. Porter and a prescription for the medication that would make her drift through each day half awake, half alive.

"What the hell is going on?" she said, startling herself by speaking the words out loud. The dead man's image replayed in her thoughts. Kerri shook her head, as if the action would be enough to scramble the likeness and crumble it to useless pieces. "I've been thinking about him too much," she determined. After all, that might be true. She hadn't slept well and she'd been through an ordeal that would make anyone edgy.

*But you're not just anyone, sweetheart,* Kerri admonished herself. *You know that. Even if you don't want to admit it, you know it.*

Kerri fell back into the landscape, forcing herself to focus on the soothing sound the water made as it moved gently. She pushed all the unpleasant thoughts away, preferring to watch the busy duck family go about their endless task of foraging for food. "I'm a little freaked by everything. You guys won't tell anyone, right?" she spoke softly as they passed her. Kerri decided that she could fit in nicely with the average duck family. She envied the easy quiet they shared. "I bet they would never think I needed to see a shrink!" she said, chuckling to herself. It felt good to be happy, if only for the briefest of moments.

It was then that she felt a hand drop on her shoulder. Kerri's panicked scream echoed across the pond.

# CHAPTER 12

**WITH ALL HER** might, Kerri thrust herself away from the weight of the hand. She fell on the sandy beach, her legs absorbing the sharp stab of the coarse pebbles. As she struggled to regain her footing, her only thought was to run. She didn't know if she was running from the dead body or from the live hand.

"Kerri, calm down. It's me." Seth was kneeling down in front of her now. His strong hands had turned her around and forced her to see his face. Recognition washed over her like a soothing balm. She leaned into Seth for a moment and then nudged him gently away. His arms gave freely, though he remained close.

"I'm sorry," she began, with a sharp exhale, "you caught me at a bad time."

"I noticed," he said without humor in his voice. He was silent for a moment then asked, "Were you thinking about last night?"

Kerri chewed her lip. She trusted Seth, but there were limits to that trust. There was no way she could tell him that she'd just seen Mark Travers floating in the pond. Seth would take one look out at the still water, see nothing, and stumble through a plausible explanation. Seth would be kind, but he wouldn't believe her.

*Who would believe me?* Kerri thought. *I just saw a dead body – a dead body that isn't really there. If I tell Seth, he'll think I'm the one who's not all there.*

"Yes," Kerri said in a shaky voice. Her heart beat overtime. It threatened to rise out of her chest and take a permanent vacation from her body. "I guess I was thinking about last night. It was pretty awful. I feel bad for the guy." She paused before adding, "I didn't hear you coming."

Seth nodded his bent head. He was busy watching his feet dig patterns in the sand, just like they had done the night before. He must have felt her watching his feet, for he straightened before asking, "So what really brings you out here?"

Kerri shrugged her shoulders, offering only a mumbled, "I don't know." She had a momentary urge to tell Seth everything, to come clean about it all. Would he treat her like a freak of nature? Not having to lie might be worth the risk.

But what about his lies? O'Connell's accusations against Seth returned full force, flooding her with an awkward guilt as though she had somehow betrayed her best friend. She glanced sideways to steal a look at Seth's face. His expression was pinched, his face exhibiting all the signs of having slept poorly or not at all. His deep brown eyes gazed at the lazy ripples in the water, allowing Kerri a moment to admire the smooth planes of his sun-darkened face. For a moment, she was stirred by the familiar wistful desire to know what their relationship had been about. Now, like a swift, sharp blow she felt a deep cleft between them, replaced by a new, surreal bond that seemed to make them more like old enemies than old friends.

"I stopped by your house," Seth said, interrupting her thoughts. "I think I woke your mom up, she seemed a tad out of it ... pissed off, too." His laughter was brief and humorless. "I don't think she knew you left the house. She mentioned something about a doctor's appointment."

"I told her I'm fine," Kerri said, firmly. "I needed to get outside. After last night, she's probably going to want me to have a police escort or something."

Seth picked up a smooth stone and skipped it across the water. "Is that why the police are at your house?"

"What? What are you talking about?" Kerri cringed at the sound of the high panic in her voice. She had done her duty by giving them her statement, so what did they want now?

"I saw my dad pull up as I was leaving." Seth's eyes were cast downward, his brows furrowed. "Everyone has to give a statement about last night, but I thought you already did that."

"I did. I went this morning. It was extremely illuminating," she said, matter-of-factly.

He stopped, mid-throw, his grip hard on the flat stone. "What do you mean by that?"

Kerri searched for what truth could be found in the dark depths of Seth's eyes. She felt that O'Connell's revelations about Seth had been akin to rolling over a rock and uncovering the dark growth that had sprung up between it and the ground. Everything they had not talked about, every reason they had not moved forward or closer together, it was all there in the space between them now.

"I mean they had quite a few questions about you, Seth. Now why do you suppose that is?" Kerri wanted to ask more. She wanted to ask Seth why he was lying to her, why he felt the need to smoke pot when it had gotten him into such trouble before, but she couldn't bring herself to ask. *Whatever we are or might be, we're still friends. If I ask him about the drugs, if I accuse him without proof, can we still be friends?*

Seth shifted, seemingly uncomfortable under her gaze. He was the first to look away.

"I might as well get it over with," Kerri said. She felt more capable now. Anger fueled her, pushed her to her feet and propelled her in the direction of her house.

"What are you going to tell them?" Seth asked, quietly.

Kerri peeked over her shoulder. Seth had not moved. What *could* she tell them? What *should* she tell them? She squared her shoulders and faced forward. "I'm going to tell them the truth of course."

*Whatever that might be.*

# CHAPTER 13

**KERRI'S SNEAKERS CRUNCHED** ungracefully on the gravel driveway. Normally, she would have taken more care, but the desire to announce her presence was spurned by the hostility that was growing within her. *I'm sick of people asking me questions that I cannot answer.* With a deep breath, she squared her shoulders and entered the house.

Dylan Roberts was seated at the kitchen table with her mother. Two coffee mugs sat empty before them on the table.

*My, he sure is comfortable, very comfortable, considering he hasn't been by here in a long time. I hope they enjoyed their cozy conversation about me.*

Their eyes crawled over her as she entered the kitchen. Kerri struggled to maintain an air of disinterest. She opened the refrigerator, grabbed a bottle of water, and began to drink it without saying a word.

"Kerri," began her mother, "Dylan wanted to talk to you about Seth. He's worried about him." Her mother's face was fixed into a practiced, plastic smile once again.

"Sure." *Give it your best shot*, she thought. She absently rubbed her temple to prevent the return of her headache. The water she had drunk sloshed uncomfortably in her empty stomach.

She took a seat at the table, noting her mother's stiff posture. *She has to be thinking about Dad*, Kerri surmised. *She has to be looking at Officer Roberts and thinking about the day he came here to tell her that Dad was never coming home again.* Kerri wondered if her mother had grown to hate the face of the man who had delivered the worst news she had ever received. Taking in the tight rigidity of his face, Kerri could understand if she had.

"Kerri, I know you're close with Seth," he began, "and I know you might think covering up for him is the same as helping him, but he's in trouble here. Can I count on your help?"

"Why are you asking *me*?" Kerri threw her hands up in anger. "Sure, I hang out with Seth a lot, but he doesn't tell me everything."

Dylan absorbed her outburst as thoroughly as a sponge laps up water. He sat patiently, as if expecting she would say more. Finally, he let out a small sigh and glanced out the kitchen window. "I'm here strictly as a father, not as a cop." He turned back toward them and slapped his open palm with his fist. "Hell, O'Connell would have a fit if he knew I was at this house. But we have a duty here. Seth needs our help. If he speaks up now, we can get him into a treatment center."

"Not jail?"

Dylan appeared incredulous. "Why do you think I'm here? I'm trying to help Seth. Last thing I want is for him to end up in prison." His hand moved down, absently tipping his empty coffee cup from side to side. "He's had a rough time lately, what with his mom gone and all." He shook his head. "Six months and not one word from her, can you believe that? She just drops off the face of the earth. Can't be helped, I guess. We have no real control over other people's actions."

Kerri lowered her head, her childish anger turning to shame. Her eye caught on Dylan's wedding ring and traced the intricately-etched design that still encircled his finger. She had dismissed Seth's loss, telling herself that his mother had the option to return. Her own pain had been paramount because the loss of her father was permanent. Now Kerri wasn't so sure that how or why a person left mattered much. Cindy Roberts had the option to be with her son, but she was as absent from Seth's life as Kerri's father was absent from hers. Maybe knowing that the missing person had a choice was worse in the end.

Kerri lifted her eyes and they locked with Dylan's. His eyes were a fierce blue, and for a moment she felt frozen, as though she could not take a breath. He broke the stare by gesturing with his head, drawing attention to the ring. "Yes, I still wear my ring. I guess I'm not able to part with it." He paused, shifting his eyes toward Kerri's mother. "I guess we have that in common." Lisa Langston nodded woodenly, briefly brushing her fingers over her diamond band before burying her hands in her lap.

"Look," Dylan cut through the ensuing silence, "O'Connell made Seth take a drug test. Seth swore to me that he hadn't done anything. But his drug test came back positive for marijuana. Now I come to find out that Seth lied in his statement. As far as I can tell, Seth could have been buying drugs from this guy, and he lied to cover it up. I think it is in his best interest if he gets away from all this and gets the help he needs."

Kerri ran an unsteady hand through her hair. "If Seth needs treatment, I want him to get it, but what can I do?"

"I need you to tell me what you saw last night. Any details you might have forgotten to mention this morning."

Kerri shook her head. "I told O'Connell everything. I ... I don't know anything else ... nothing for sure." Her throat went dry. Her mouth felt as if it were filled with dust.

Her mother was looking at her, alarmed. "Kerri, are you okay? My God, you look like you've seen a ghost or something." For a moment, recognition flashed across her face, but it was gone in an instant, fading like a specter into the air.

Dylan leaned forward. "Kerri, what are you trying to say? Are you saying you do know something, but you're not sure if you should mention it? Because what we should be thinking about right now is Seth. He is in serious trouble here."

"Serious trouble? I know he violated his probation, but it's not like they caught him with drugs, right?"

"No, but they caught him in a lie. Just think about it. Lying to the police, in the middle of a homicide investigation? Hell, that spells bad news any way you look at it – even if your father is on the squad," Dylan said firmly. "There's only so much I can do to protect him." He ran a forceful hand over his shortly-cropped hair, his silver wedding ring flashing intermittently as it caught and reflected the light above the table. He leaned back into his chair. "Your father was an officer. You know how this works. Seth knew this guy. How do you think it's going to look? Seth knows the victim, when no one else knows a thing about him except that he's a recluse? How long do you think it will be before he's listed as a suspect? Then it won't matter if he violated his probation. I won't be able to help him then."

"And I don't know how to help him now," she said, hollowly, as she watched tears trace a line down her mother's broken face.

# CHAPTER 14

**KERRI SET TWO** plates at the table, folding the paper napkins with more care than necessary. She looked at her mother, who was busily stirring at the stove. *Turn around*, Kerri said silently to her mother's back. *Talk about what happened this afternoon!* But her mother only tapped her spoon against the side of the pan and placed it on the spoon rest.

"Dinner smells good, Mom."

"Mm hmm," her mother murmured. She didn't look up. Instead, she filled bowls and plates and brought them to the table. When she was done, she took off her apron and folded it carefully. "Time to eat," she said.

Kerri slid into her chair, but her mother's tension was so palpable that it caused Kerri's every movement to become stiff and awkward in an effort to be silent. Kerri pushed the food around her plate. She was hungry, but was unable to eat in front of her mother. She opened her mouth to speak, her throat rusty and unused. Realizing that she had nothing to say, she cleared her throat as quietly as possible.

"Finish your dinner," her mother said, absently nodding toward Kerri's plate before resuming her empty stare.

Kerri stilled the nervous movements of her fork. "You know that I can't help it, right? I mean, it's not like I have any control of it." Her pleading made her sick with frustration.

Her mother looked up, confused, as if she had awakened from a long sleep. "What do you mean, Kerri?"

"I think you know what I mean." She let her fork fall. It clanged loudly against her plate. "I see what I see. I can't help that sometimes it shows me things that might be all wrong. I know it was bad before, with Dad, I mean. I know that it's still bad. God, you have never even unpacked his stuff from his desk at work!" She paused, trying hard to be gentle. "Listen, I don't want to see you go through it all again, but we have to deal with this, right?"

Her mother let out a long sigh. She turned her tired eyes to Kerri. "We've dealt with it, Kerri. You gave your statement to the police, and now they can do their job." She stood up and began clearing the full dinner plates off the table.

*Oh, no. Not again*, Kerri thought as she stood up and followed her mother into the kitchen. "But you know I didn't tell them everything! Aren't you going to ask me what I really saw?"

Her mother put a plate down. She motioned for quiet with her hands, as she probably had done a million times as a school teacher to a rowdy bunch of kindergarteners. "Listen, Kerri, I don't pretend to know what goes on in your head. I know you see ... " she paused, closing her eyes briefly and shaking her head in defeat. "Whatever it is, I think it is best to stick with the facts. We'll all be better off."

Kerri felt the anger rising. "Oh, and I'll be better off with a mother who thinks I'm crazy, who thinks I need to see Dr. Porter? Is this going to be like last time? Gee, get the hysterical girl some tranquilizers, then she won't bother us all with those pesky visions of her dead father – "

"That's enough!" her mother shouted. Her face was flushed, her eyes snapped in anger. "I might not have always known the right thing to do, Kerri, but I hardly treat you like you're insane. And I won't tolerate you treating me like a ... a drug-pushing tyrant. I did what I thought was best." She turned toward the sink, her back a ridged wall between them.

Kerri stared at her mother's back and watched her arms move as they rinsed the dinner dishes. The sting of bitter tears flooded her eyes and she blurted out, "I do think you did what you thought was best – best for you."

# CHAPTER 15

**IN THE QUIET** of her room, Kerri gave in to her aching heart. Her chest clenched in a twisted knot wound so tight that although her shoulders heaved with the force of her crying, she made almost no sound. Falling to her knees, she curled into a protective ball and buried her face in her hands. A ragged breath tore through her as she squeezed against the pain, willing her tears not to fall.

She sought out her father's picture. Brushing away the moisture from her eyes, she carefully picked up the frame and sat on the edge of her bed. "We're not doing great without you, Dad," she whispered, with a shaky smile, "nope, not so great." It was an average photograph, but the normalcy of it was why she cherished it. Her father, at the grill, wearing his favorite, faded baseball hat, a shiny metal spatula clutched in his hand that lay folded across his chest. But it was his smile that Kerri loved the most. It was a smile that came too easy not to be genuine.

How could he smile like that if he wasn't happy? *People smile for pictures,* she reminded herself, *but some smiles are only lies.*

*Like Seth's smile?* She put the picture down and lay back on the bed, letting out a deep sigh and staring sightlessly at the ceiling. *What am I going to do about Seth?* Kerri could not believe that the police could possibly think Seth could be a murderer.

*God,* she thought. *Murderers are inhuman monsters. They are not best friends who laugh at your jokes. And definitely not guys you've thought about kissing.*

*Besides,* Kerri reasoned, *Seth was with me all night. Even if I thought he was capable of doing something like this, he was there with me, right?*

*Except he wasn't next to me all night, was he? Seth had left the party. Yes,* she thought, *he went with Mike. They were supposed to get marshmallows and hotdogs to roast over the fire, but they ended up coming back with beer.*

They never said how they got it, although Mike was close to the legal age. He probably had a fake ID that he picked up on his campus.

She rolled over to her side, glancing back at her father's picture. It was hard to believe a time had existed when she had felt secure, when her father's presence was all she needed to feel safe. *Dad,* she pleaded silently, *I need you. Wherever you are, I need you to give me the strength to deal with this.* His face became blurry as her eyes filled with unshed tears.

"I'll keep trying to see what happened to you, Dad. I

promise," she whispered, "no matter what." She could not give up. No matter how many times she wished for her visions to cease, she could not let her father down by quitting. *I wish I would see what I need to see*, she thought. It always felt as though something was blocking her from seeing the truth. Was it herself?

Reaching her arm out, she gently clasped the picture and brought it closer. She hoped her father was happy wherever he was now. She prayed that he was not disappointed in her. For a while after he had died, she had felt him everywhere. She would turn around, half expecting him to be there, yet seeing only the emptiness.

Once, she had a dream – an ordinary dream – that had told her that his death had been a big mistake. Kerri had awakened elated, only to have reality crash down on her, ripping open her wounded heart with a pain that was raw and new.

Kerri stared at her father's still likeness, saying for the thousandth time, "I'm sorry, Dad." His sandy blond hair poked out from under his worn baseball cap, and his olive-colored eyes twinkled. He smiled back, carelessly, a man with no worries, with all the time in the world. She started to put the picture back on her nightstand, a shaky hand swiping away the wetness that was now under her eyes.

For a moment, Kerri smiled back at her father, feeling his presence cover her like a warm, comfortable blanket. She didn't want to move, fearing any little thing would break the feeling. She clutched the picture tightly to her chest. She closed her eyes for a minute, savored the brief connection. When she opened her eyes, she whispered a quiet, "Thank you," smiling back at the glossy image.

Suddenly, Kerri was no longer looking at her father. Instead, Mark Travers's dead face floated over her father's face. Kerri dropped the frame. It landed face up, bouncing on the soft surface of her bed. Her hands clenched her cheeks, and she could hear the rapid breaths escaping from her open mouth. "No," she whispered, but the image had already vanished, leaving Kerri to question which dead man had provided her with a fleeting gift of solace and which had taken it away.

# CHAPTER 16

**KERRI WAS ABOUT** to hang up, when Ann answered the phone on the third ring. "Hello?"

"Ann, can I come over?"

"What's wrong?"

"Nothing's wrong – "

"Yeah, right." Ann laughed. "Do you realize that you only come over here when something is wrong? Not that I mind."

"Mom and I had a fight. I saw ... I don't want to talk about it over the phone. Can you pick me up? I'm not about to ask Mom for the car keys right now."

"Sure. I'll be there in fifteen minutes." Kerri hung up the phone and quietly slipped past her mother's closed bedroom door. She jotted a quick note saying where she'd be and sat on the porch to wait. Before long, Ann's battered grey sedan eased into the driveway. Kerri leaped to her feet, opening the door to take a seat before Ann had put the car in park.

"Anxious?" Ann asked, one eyebrow rising in a quizzical arch.

"It shows that much?" The corner of her mouth lifted into a half-hearted smile.

Ann pulled away from the house, keeping up a steady chatter about her waitress job at the Golden Sunrise Diner. Kerri didn't know how Ann had the energy to work early morning shifts and go nights to the local community college. When she had asked her how she managed it all, Ann shrugged, saying that she never gave it much thought.

Ann's modest three-room apartment was right above the diner. It boasted a decent-sized bedroom and a tiny bathroom, but the biggest area was entirely open, serving as both a living room and kitchen. A worn uniform was strewn over a dinette chair.

"Come on in. Excuse the mess," Ann said. "Want me to make coffee?" Acknowledging Kerri's nodding head, she went to work. "Have a seat."

Kerri plopped down on the lumpy second-hand couch. "Do you have class tonight?"

"No. I decided not to take any summer classes." She gave Kerri a sideways grin. "Or I should say that my checkbook decided that I'd sit out for the summer." She rolled her eyes dramatically. "Sorry, all I have is instant."

After Ann boiled the water and made the coffee, she handed Kerri a steaming mug, the tiny brown flecks still floating on the surface. Grimacing at the bitter taste, she spooned in some sugar. "It's the same thing as it always is, Ann, except now it isn't only about Dad." She slammed her mug down. Coffee spilled onto the table. "Why can't she ever talk about him?"

"I think she can't talk about Dad because ... " she paused, contemplating her words as she used a paper towel to mop up the coffee. "Because talking about him makes it real. Do you know what I mean? As long as Mom doesn't say it out loud, it's like he isn't really gone."

"I never thought about it like that before. You're probably right. She still hasn't gone through his things. It's been three years, and his clothes are still in the closet! And today, when Officer Roberts showed up – "

"What was *he* doing at the house?" Ann interrupted, an edge creeping into her voice.

"He wanted to talk about Seth." Kerri ran her fingers through her hair. "Seth is in trouble. He failed his drug test and he lied to the police about how he knew this dead guy, Mark. A guy who, I might add, was growing pot. For all I know, Mark was the one selling Seth drugs. The police are going to think that because Seth lied, he might have been capable of killing this guy. And now I can't bring myself to trust Seth anymore, but that's crazy right?"

Ann's finger tapped her mug. "Listen, I know you and Seth have always been tight, but he's changed."

"You can't think that Seth has changed so much that he could kill someone?" Kerri said incredulously. "Come on!"

"No, but Seth hasn't been the same since his mother

took off. Does anyone even know why she left or where she is for that matter? It must bother him. Maybe that's why he's doing drugs." She paused, quietly adding, "Ever since Dad, I don't feel the same way I did toward the Roberts family. I know they came over to our house and checked on us, for a while anyway. They did their duty, I guess, but every time I would hear Dylan say that he wished he could have stopped Dad from firing the gun, I wanted to smash his face. I didn't want to hear that. I still don't." Ann's eyes welled up and she turned her head away.

"Ann," Kerri murmured, placing her hand on Ann's arm.

Ann squeezed Kerri's hand, swallowed hard, and took a shuddery breath. "Shit, this never really gets any easier, does it?"

Kerri shook her head. "No. People say stupid things when someone dies. They don't know what to say, but they feel they have to say something. Dylan is no exception. And he might honestly feel like it's his fault."

"He wouldn't be the only one," Ann snapped. "Sorry, Kerri, this is ancient history, I know. It just makes me so mad!" Ann threw her hands out and slammed them on the table hard enough to make the spoons in their coffee mugs clang. "I don't think I would feel this way if, just once, Dylan had said that Dad wasn't the kind of man that would kill himself, if he had given me some sign that showed he was as shocked as we were, but no, instead Dylan heaps his own guilt onto us. Honestly, I was glad when they stopped coming by. I don't think Dylan Roberts did right by any of us."

"Listen, you can't blame Dylan for not saving Dad any more that you can blame Seth for what his father has done throughout this whole thing."

Ann groaned. She blew out a rush of hot air from her lips. "No, you're right, but the Roberts are not my top priority. I'm much more concerned about you right now."

Kerri chewed her bottom lip. "It's not Seth or the fight with Mom. It's something more."

"I thought so. What did you see?"

"I keep thinking about the dead guy, Mark. I keep seeing his face." As objectively as she could, Kerri related the events of the past couple of days to Ann. When she finished, Kerri searched Ann's face for skepticism, but found her merely clenching her eyebrows as she formed a question.

"What was Seth doing at Deacon Pond?"

"I told you. There was a party," Kerri answered.

"No, not the night you found the body, but today? I mean, if he was being questioned by the police, and they had suspicions that he was involved in the drugs that were found, the police would hold him, right?"

Kerri hadn't thought about that. "Well, his dad could have pulled some strings? Said he could be remanded into his custody at a later time?"

"Sure, but you'd think they would have plenty to talk about, right? Or that Seth would be laying low. Instead, he's following you down to the beach, while his father is pumping Mom for information. Something doesn't add up."

"Seth was as freaked out as I was," Kerri suggested. "He might have simply wanted to see how I was holding up, or if I was going to be able to help him."

Ann sat quietly for a few moments, fingertips patting against her coffee mug. "Maybe Seth was only keeping an eye on you, looking out for you like friends do," Ann said, agreeably, before her tone hardened, "but Kerri, think about it. Seth's smoking pot again. So that means he is involved in drugs – possibly with the drugs they found on Mark's property – a man he lied about how he knew. Now Mark is dead, and I'm betting that the police have added up these strikes against Seth already."

"No," Kerri whispered.

"Hey," Ann said, shrugging her shoulders, "I think Seth was probably buying drugs off Mark and lied to cover it up. But, I also think it's possible that the two of them were partners, selling the stuff. Mark might have gotten greedy, threatened to go to the police if Seth didn't hand over the profits."

"Why would Seth risk getting involved in all that?" Kerri said. "His father is a cop. That would be crazy. And, even if he was, you can't believe that Seth would kill someone? We've known Seth forever. Our families have been connected our whole lives. Birthday parties, picnics, days at the beach – it's ridiculous to think he would be capable of something like this."

"Is it?" Ann asked. "How can you know how

someone will react when they've been backed into a corner, when they think they have no choice? If Seth was being blackmailed, he might have felt desperate. Maybe Seth didn't mean to hurt Mark." Ann reached over and touched Kerri's hand. "I'm sorry. I know you don't want to hear this, but you have to. Innocent people don't lie, and make no mistake – Seth is hiding something. I'd have to say that whatever the truth is, Seth knows more than he's saying. I bet he followed you to the beach to find out if you knew more than you were saying too."

"I don't know anything," Kerri said, stunned by everything Ann had just said. "Seth has no idea about my ... gift."

"Don't be too sure about that," Ann said.

"What do you mean?"

"I mean this is a small town with a small police station. Dylan was Dad's partner. I know people forget things, but a kid who disputes a police report because of a psychic vision? No, you don't get that everyday. I think you'd remember that."

Kerri's arms bristled with goose bumps. *Was it possible? Had Seth known, all this time, about her visions? And if he did, why would he risk lying to her?*

Kerri shivered. She felt cold; colder than when she'd huddled under the thin police blanket, staring at Mark's dead body; colder still than she'd felt on the day her father had died. *How could I be so foolish? Of course Seth knows about my visions. But that's not important now,* Kerri thought. *What is important is finding out what Seth is hiding.*

# Chapter 17

KERRI HAD NO idea why she was so nervous to go into the Shop N' Save later that week. While customers buzzed in and out of the swinging, automatic doors, Kerri stood back. *I'm going to pick up my last paycheck. It's mine. I'm entitled to it.* Still, she hesitated.

She groaned and rolled her eyes. *God, I can't even lie to myself! Okay, I'll admit it. I want to check out Seth's file.*

The air conditioning instantly blasted the sweat off her body when she stepped inside. *All right, so now I'm one cool crook, one chilly criminal, one ...*

"Hey, Kerri, what brings you here?" White teeth flashed in a friendly smile.

"Hi, Stacy," she said, in a rush. "I'm here to get my check. How are things?"

"Not bad ... I feel really awful, though, about taking your hours. If you want to come back, I'll be glad to – "

"No, don't worry about it." She waved her hand and

smiled, trying to smooth over the awkwardness. "It's just a job, right?"

"Well, if you change your mind, let me know. In the meantime, checks are in the office, same place as always. Go on in, Bob is out again – lunch or something. Who knows? He's been out a lot lately."

"Thanks. I'm in a rush, so I'll just grab my check and go, okay?"

"Sure thing." Stacy was already heading toward the employee break room.

*While the cat's away, the mice will take long breaks.* Kerri waited a beat before slipping into the silence of the office. Her hand hovered over the envelope that held their checks. She glanced conspicuously over her shoulder before she pulled open the metal filing cabinet, fingers swiftly pulling back the alphabet tabs, until she reached Roberts. She tossed another look over her shoulder and then pulled out Seth's file. She flipped past his application and work papers, looking for his delivery sheets.

They weren't there. Why were they missing? *I need to find that record. I know O'Connell told me the police already looked for them, but I have to try. It's the only way to prove that Seth is telling the truth about the deliveries he made to Mark.* Defeated, she slid the folder back, her fingers drumming on the cool metal.

"What do you think you're doing?" Bob boomed from the doorway.

"Oh, Bob," she blurted out. "I – I was just getting my

check ... you called me, remember? You said – "

"I know what I said, and I didn't give you permission to go poking around in people's files." He pointed toward the envelope on the counter. "Your check is in there, same as always. Now get your check and get out of here."

Kerri's fingers shook as she looked through the pile of checks for her own. Her shallow breaths cut through the silence. At last she found her check, and she carefully placed the envelope back on the counter. Under Bob's cold scrutiny, she managed to squeak out a pathetic "good-bye," before closing the door on his gruff, non-verbal reply.

"Caveman," she muttered behind the safety of the closed door. She left quickly, grateful she would have no reason to ever return. "Thanks, Mom," she whispered, meaning it for the first time in a long time.

# CHAPTER 18

**THE DAY WAS** overcast, but the glare was so strong it made Kerri squint her eyes hard enough to hurt. She ducked into the cool, grey garage. She had spent the last few days all alone. She didn't trust herself to be normal around anyone in such a constant state of flux, for one moment was spent in turmoil, the next retreating safely to utter blankness. She wished she could clear her head of every thought, every vision that had ever entered her mind, but it was impossible. She could no more forget the visions she had than she could forget the people who appeared in them.

*Why am I here again? Why can't I leave it alone?* She had entered the garage without any real intentions, yet there in front of her was the box containing her father's office things. Kerri had always been drawn to the box. But since tripping on Mark Travers's lifeless body, she found herself passing by it several times daily without having the guts to take it down off the shelf. *God*, she thought, *I'm just as scared as Mom.* Kerri chewed on her lip, taking yet another backward glance before reaching up to slide the box down. "Screw it," she muttered. "I have to look."

She hesitated as her hands were about to unfold the cardboard flaps. She checked for movement at the back door. *If Mom catches me ...*

She shook her head, not wanting to think about how her mother would react. Instead, she tugged at the opening, inhaling the faint musty smell of dampness and age. The contents were in disarray, as though they were packed with haste. Briefly, Kerri registered bright smiling faces in family photos and a set of street clothes that were rumpled and unkempt.

Normally she would have cherished these items, held on to them as a valuable link to her father, but now, Kerri pushed these items impatiently aside. She felt rushed, far less disturbed by the possibility that her mother would discover her looting, than by the pressing feeling that she was supposed to find something and had failed to do so – something specific that she could not name or recognize until it was within her grasp. She let out a frustrated breath. Her eye caught upon something shiny. Her fingers dug, clenching cool metal. For a minute, it snagged on something, but she gave an extra tug and it pulled free, still attached to her father's uniform shirt.

*Dad's badge*, she thought, running a shaky hand over the gold star, feeling the bumps and grooves of the engraved letters. *Dad loved being a cop*, she thought. *He'd always make sure the dry cleaners used extra starch when they pressed his uniform – that's how proud he was to wear it. This crumpled shirt – this wasn't Dad at all.*

She pulled her father's shirt close to her and hugged it to her body. She smelled the cloth, hoping to catch the lingering scent of his Old Spice aftershave, but the shirt smelled dank and mildewed.

*Dad always wore Old Spice, said he liked it. But then again, he didn't really have a choice. We'd buy it for him every year for his birthday.*

Kerri folded his shirt carefully, as though her father were going to wear it tomorrow. The badge was displayed on top and she gave it a quick shine with the bottom of her T-shirt. *There. That's better. Nice and neat like Dad always liked it.*

She saw another uniform shirt and she plunged deeper in the box to retrieve it. *What a wrinkled mess,* Kerri thought. *And so dirty!* But as she pulled out the rumpled shirt, she realized that it wasn't dirt. *It's blood,* she thought. *Dad's blood – this must have been the shirt he was wearing when –*

Kerri choked back her tears and began to straighten the shirt as best she could. As she smoothed the shirt with her hand, she felt a lump in the breast pocket. Kerri slid her fingers inside, pulling out another police badge. It was identical to her father's, except for the name imprinted across the metal. "Roberts," she whispered.

"What are you doing?"

Kerri jumped, her hand releasing the badge. She

heard the clatter as it fell to the floor, and she quickly closed the box flaps. Seth stood before her, his hands stuffed into the pockets of his baggy shorts. Kerri shrugged, not wanting him to see that she was scared. She turned to stuff the box back on the shelf. "I was looking for Ann's old high school journal. You know, from Mrs. Johnston's class." Her eye located the gold badge.

"Oh. Why do you want that?"

"I'm going to have her this year, and I thought it might help." Kerri shrugged. "Ann said she was a good teacher, but tough. It's good to be prepared, right?" Kerri was surprised by how effortlessly the lie had formed. *I guess I'm not a bad liar after all.*

"I think you dropped something."

"Yeah," she said as she bent down to scoop up the badge and put it in her pocket, "only a hair clip."

Seth nodded. "Your mom said you were in the backyard." He shuffled his feet, making scratching noises on the cement. "I don't think she knew you were out here."

*Why did he say that?* She nibbled on her lip, turning her head away. *Did he know she'd secretly been looking in her father's things?* Her hands became restless. She shoved them in her pockets. *At least Mom doesn't know.*

Seth glanced back at the closed door that connected the garage to the mud room. "Can we talk?"

"Sure," Kerri said, trying to act normally. It was on the tip of her tongue to ask him what he wanted to talk about, but she clamped her mouth shut. They only had one thing to talk about anymore.

Seth found two old milk crates and turned them over to serve as make-shift seats. He sat down, waiting for Kerri to follow suit. Their limbs shifted in response to the awkward silence that grew between them. "Listen, I'm sorry. I didn't want to involve you in my lies," Seth burst out. "Sometimes things start off one way and you think you're not hurting anyone or you don't mean to ... " he trailed off. Kerri felt him search her face for a response.

The familiar pull was there, and she had the momentary urge to grab his hand, to hold it and tell him they would both be fine, but she held back. *Touching sometimes tells me more than I want to know.*

Instead, she did her best to push away the anger that burned in the pit of her stomach. *He's making a step toward me. I have to meet him halfway.*

"I suppose I can see why you might not have talked to me," she said. "But I guess I still wish you had."

"I want to tell you things. Really, there is so much that I can't talk about with anyone."

"Seth, we're friends, right? We should be able to help each other, be there for each other." She plunged ahead. "This whole thing makes me wonder. I don't want to feel like this, but I can't help but wonder about what other lies you might have told, you know? It's like Ann said – "

"Ann? What's she got to do with any of this?" Seth said with a hardness to his voice.

"Ann said that you probably lied about Mark because you didn't want people to know how you knew him."

"Ann," he ground out, "should mind her own damn business. She doesn't know what she's talking about."

"Well," Kerri began, "if Ann's so wrong, why don't you set things right? Why don't you tell me the truth about Mark and the pot and everything else you've been lying about?" A slow, sick feeling crept into the pit of her stomach. *Do I really want to know? Am I ready to hear what he has to say?*

"You're not interested in the truth. You're too pissed off to listen to anything I have to say. And as far as Ann goes – "

"What about Ann?"

"Ann's just trying to turn you against me. That's why she's spouting off with this bullshit story. She's full of crap!"

"How can you say that?" Kerri repeated, growing angry. "No, Seth, you're wrong. I trust Ann. She's always been truthful, unlike some people I know."

"Well, what about you? You don't exactly tell me what's going on with you!" Seth sat up, his back a rigid line.

"What are you talking about?"

"I mean my father told me all about you! He told me how you think you *see* things." He motioned like a child talking about the boogeyman. "Tell me, Kerri, what do you see right now?"

His mocking spurned an instant surge of anger within her. She wanted to tell him to go to hell, that he was a pathetic loser that she never wanted to set her eyes upon again, but she couldn't bring herself to say it. She wanted to ask Seth why he'd lied about Mark, she wanted to hear him say that there was no way he could have killed him. She wanted to hear it and believe it in her heart. But she couldn't say any of it because she was afraid she would never see him again as a result. *I've already lost Dad. I don't think I could stand to lose Seth too.*

Anger pricked at her, the way the badge's sharp points stabbed her leg through the thin lining of her shorts. She had waited so long, hoping that Seth would one day see her for who she was, who she could be. *Listen to him! He thinks I'm a joke. He'll never see me as a normal girl. To him, I'm a circus freak.*

*So*, her inner voice argued back, *you might as well stick up for yourself. It's time. You can't lose Seth, because you never really had him to begin with.*

A calm certainty began to steal over her. She wasn't going to hang her head anymore. "You know, Seth, didn't anyone ever tell you not to judge things you don't understand? Right now, all I see is a scared little boy who isn't even remotely ready to comprehend the likes of the person standing right in front of him." Before Seth could shake off the stunned look he wore on his face, Kerri walked away, leaving him alone in the garage. Each step Kerri took made her feel better than she had in a long time.

# CHAPTER 19

**EVEN BEHIND HER** dark sunglasses, the brilliant, mid-morning sun made Kerri's eyes involuntarily squeeze tighter. She stopped to take a sip of water, trying to get her bearings on the unfamiliar trail. To make her mother more comfortable, Kerri was hiking through Deacon Pond's more popular section, but Kerri wasn't sure it made much of a difference. The serious fishermen would have left hours before and the beach traffic was light during the week. *Besides, it's a pond. It's one big circle.* Still, she had not been on this side of the pond in a long time. It made her uneasy to glance upon objects that were wholly foreign. *Great, watch me get lost after trying to convince Mom that I'd be perfectly safe!*

Kerri rested on a felled tree, which was perfumed with the moist, rotten smell that invaded her nostrils. No matter how far she walked or how much summer sun she soaked up, Kerri could not escape the gloom inside her.

At times she felt convinced that a mundane reason was hiding somewhere for Dylan Roberts's badge to be packed away with her father's uniform. Yet other times Kerri thought it might mean something more. She reached inside her roomy pocket to pull out the golden-bronze badge. Her fingers smoothed across the metal, feeling nothing except the carved letters. *If it meant something, I would feel it, right?* There was no answer to her silent question.

She quickly replaced the badge, feeling the awkward shape against her thigh. The feeling of Kerri's initial triumph over Seth had long since evaporated. It wasn't long before she was plagued by a nagging assumption that she had been far too harsh with him.

*Even if I felt I had to be a bit heavy-handed, I should have tried to find out what he meant about Ann,* she thought. *Why would Seth think Ann would be trying to turn me against him?* Kerri had been so far off about Seth's troubles. It wasn't a stretch to think she might have missed something about Ann as well. *Some psychic I'm turning out to be,* she lamented. *I thought I was the one who was supposed to see what other people can't.*

Even as she berated herself, Kerri knew it wasn't all her fault. *How can I blame myself for not using my sight, when I've been encouraged my whole life to pretend it doesn't exist?* She didn't know how it worked because she had spent so much time and effort wishing it away. She thought about Petey then. She had spent many afternoons chasing him. But after that first day she'd seen him after he died, remembering the way her mother had acted, she had kept her visions to herself.

But one day she and Ann had been playing hide-and-seek after Petey died. Being older, Ann was always tough to find. She'd squeeze into impossibly small spaces or scale tree branches, knowing full well which ones Kerri would never be able to climb. That day, Ann had hidden behind an old wood shed – far out of the designated hiding area. But Kerri had found her. Petey had shown her the way.

"How did you find me?" Ann had asked, amazed.

Kerri refused to answer. Finally, Ann had tackled her to the ground, tickling Kerri until she was on the verge of tears. "All right," Kerri had gasped. "Petey showed me."

"Really? Can you see Petey now?"

"No, he comes and goes."

Ann had nodded, in awe. She'd made Kerri promise to tell her the next time Petey came. "I want to see him too."

Kerri had made good on the promise, but Ann hadn't been able to see him, no matter how hard she tried. Kerri had wanted more than anything to have Ann see Petey, to share the special time with him, but when it had become obvious that Ann would never see him, Kerri had begun to wish Petey wouldn't come. In the years that followed, Petey did not come as often. It was almost as if he'd heard Kerri's wish. He seemed only to come when Kerri was feeling sad or lonely, as if he sensed when she needed him most.

*But that changed after Dad died*, Kerri thought. She

would have liked to have seen Petey then, but he wouldn't come to her anymore, and she didn't know how to make him appear. "It's not like I ever tried to control it or force it to come," she whispered. "Why would I?"

*Yes, why?* It was a crazy idea. Yet if ever there was a time to try, it was now. If she could control this thing, it would change everything! She would no longer have to be afraid.

Kerri's heart was racing wildly, fueled by fear and hope. *I could try it. Who has to know if it doesn't work? Well, I'll know, for one,* she thought, *but God – I have to give it a shot.*

"If it works, no more hiding," she spoke softly. "No more excuses."

Kerri glanced around, but she was completely alone in the woods. As she walked farther, Kerri supposed that she had known all along that she had been approaching Mark Travers's property. Did his presence draw her there, like a moth to a flame? Underneath the fear lay a perverse comfort that made her feel as if she were among friends. *Dead friends,* she thought, shaking her head at the absurdity. Yet ever since she had seen Mark's face layered over her father's face, she had felt a strange connection that told her that he was not out to hurt her.

Instead, Kerri had begun to wonder if it was possible that Mark also had something that he wanted her to see. Was it mere coincidence that made Mark's face materialize over her father's?

*Do I feel like I'm getting to know Mark or do I just feel*

*safer because I think he's somehow connected to Dad? That might not even be the case,* she thought, *and it might be dangerous to let my guard down.*

Looking up, Kerri saw that she was standing at the base of the steep cliff where Mark had fallen. She shuddered, recalling their shared memory. Her hand reached out to touch a boulder's craggy surface. Kerri closed her eyes against the light breeze and warm summer sun. She stood there, waiting and fearing what might come next, yet there was nothing except the jagged surface of the sun-baked rock.

"I'll have to get up there," she whispered. It took her half an hour to find safe passage. Thorns scratched tracks on her legs. Tiny grey burrs covered her sneakers and socks. Sweaty, she stopped at the peak to survey the remnants of the marijuana field. A forgotten yellow tape thread waved wildly in the wind. "Do Not Cross," it read.

*Here we go.* She walked cautiously closer to the edge, peeking over despite the sick feeling it gave her stomach. A gust of wind moved her upper torso forward, scaring her enough to move backward. "God," she said aloud. "It's so creepy." *Despite the beautiful view of the pond, the cool breeze and peaceful quiet, it's just plain creepy.*

Kerri walked around. She touched anything she thought Mark might have touched, but she felt nothing except the generic sadness of a lost life. *The man may have done nothing wrong, but of course, I don't know that.* The thought drew Kerri into the marijuana field. Her feet passed by unearthed and broken roots as well as the brown and deadened remains from the plants that had been sprayed by the police.

Kerri tried to concentrate. For the first time in her life, she hoped for a vision. She touched a lifeless leaf. It crumbled to pieces and scattered in the breeze. "There is nothing here," she said in a hollow voice.

She pushed her hair out of her face with a frustrated sigh. *This is useless.* She forced a small smile in order to combat her disappointment. *Well, I tried. That has to count for something, right?*

She took a few more steps, gazing at the house in the distance. *He must have been nuts, living out here, so far from town. But, then again, if you have something to hide ... maybe it's smart.*

Still, Kerri couldn't imagine stepping one foot inside that house. There was something so spooky about it. It was like a fat spider that dropped down from the ceiling on a thin, silk thread and dangled inches above the naked skin of the person below. It was like the feel of the hairy legs as they crawled across the flesh, scampering to get away.

*But it's where Mark lived. It's where the clues will be ...*

She took a few more steps, slowly, reluctantly. "I can't do this," she said aloud. "Not by myself. No way." She stopped short of some low bushes. Though the day was warm, she felt goose bumps rise up on her skin. She brushed her palms up and down her arms to ward them away.

"What's this?" she said, bending down to look inside

the bush in front of her. "A barrette," she whispered, reaching out to grasp the metal clip. She turned it over in her hands. *What a strange shape for a barrette,* she thought, tracing the pattern that looked like a sideways eight. "It's the infinity symbol, I think." There were stray hairs left near the clasp, as though it had been pulled off without being opened.

*Well she's a blonde, whoever she is,* Kerri thought. *She's probably some cute cheerleader who came up here to make out with her boyfriend. It happens all the time around this place. Not that I'd know.*

For a moment, Kerri felt jealous of this nameless, faceless girl, but something about the barrette made her turn cold. She wanted to toss it into the woods, to pretend that she'd never seen it.

Kerri closed her eyes and fell into darkness. Something was coming. Her wrists burned. Her shoulders ached. Her clothes were wet and putrid. Her arms were pinned behind her. Her legs were stuck together. She kicked weakly in the darkness, trying to roll over. She knew she should get up, but she was so, so tired.

"Don't," a voice called out to her. "He'll hurt you again."

"Who are you?" she asked.

"Nobody – anymore."

Kerri opened her eyes. Suddenly it was all gone. She was back in the field again, grasping the barrette as though it were a lifeline. *What was that? Where was I? Did it have anything to do with Mark?* Kerri curled her hand around the barrette. *It belongs to a girl, but not a perky cheerleader. It belongs to a girl who has lost hope, to a girl who's tied up and in pain.*

"This is crazy. What did I think I could do? I shouldn't – "

"Be here? Yeah, what do you think you're doing?" a strong voice suddenly boomed behind her.

Kerri whipped around to find herself face-to-face with Seth's father, Officer Roberts.

# CHAPTER 20

"**I DON'T THINK** you answered my question, Kerri. What do you think you are doing, walking around my crime scene?" Dylan Roberts folded his hands across his broad chest with the appearance of a man who could hold out as long as it took to get the answers he wanted.

Kerri's eyes darted from place to place as though they could find no safe object to fall upon. Her hand unwittingly felt for the badge hidden inside her pocket, but shrunk away from it when she felt Roberts's cool gaze following her movements. "I was ... I was walking. I didn't mean – "

"To disturb the crime scene? Luckily, we've collected what we need, but you should know better than anyone how important it is to preserve the integrity of the scene." He shook his head, solemnly appearing to marvel at her stupidity. "Of course now I'll have to let O'Connell know about your presence here today. It won't take a genius to figure out what he'll make of you trespassing on a crime scene, interfering with a police investigation."

"I wasn't trespassing," Kerri asserted, weakly, but she could imagine what O'Connell would say. He'd tell her that tampering with evidence was a criminal offense, that she could be arrested for obstruction of justice. Kerri saw her distorted tiny likeness reflected back in Dylan's mirrored sunglasses.

"Oh, no?" His muscles flexed as he tilted his head back. "It sure looks like trespassing to me, but maybe you'd like the opportunity to explain yourself. What do you think, Kerri? You can talk to me right now, or I can explain it all to O'Connell later. I'm sure you've been looking forward to having a nice visit with him again. Your choice, Kerri."

Kerri licked her lips nervously. *Why did I come here? Why did I think this was a good idea?* "Listen," she began, "I was hoping I could find something to help Seth. I didn't mean any harm. In fact, I hardly touched anything." Kerri forced herself to look directly at him for as long as she could, but compared to him, she was as small as a bug under a microscope.

Dylan Roberts slowly removed his sunglasses, folded them carefully, and placed them in his front pocket next to his police badge. The badge caught the sunlight, briefly reflecting the light in a blinding flash. As Dylan took a step toward her, Kerri reflexively caressed the badge in her pocket, wondering again why it had been in her father's box. *It was most likely misplaced*, she thought, but that only meant it was unintentional. *Roberts would have known that it was missing. He would have had to ask for a new one. He would have wondered where it went.*

"I'm sure you want to help Seth, but I'm not sure that what you're up to is the kind of help he needs." He leaned in closer and added, "You wouldn't be trying something like before, would you now? Because you know that didn't turn out so well for your father, Kerri. Let's face it, I can't have you messing things up for me like that."

Kerri stood frozen, breathing in only shallow tracts of air. The badge on his chest was only a foot away from her now, and she had to suppress an urge to reach out and touch it. She closed her eyes for a moment to block the view, but she continued to see its image as though it were burned into her mind.

"It's good we understand each other, Kerri," Roberts said as he moved away from her. "This isn't a good place for you to be. It's dangerous. Just look at that drop," he said, pointing. "No, I'd say you don't belong here at all. Wouldn't you agree?"

"I was trying to help Seth," she repeated.

"You can help by being a friend, by convincing him that going to rehab is what's best. Leave the investigation to me," he said sternly. He pointed to the badge at his chest. "I'm the law. Do you understand?"

Kerri felt her head nod slowly. She saw his lean fingers tap the gold badge, but they moved in slow motion. Although Dylan's lips were moving, time was suspended. Kerri saw a hand reach out, a masculine hand with scant dark hair and a plain gold wedding band encircling one finger. *Dad. That looks like Dad's ring.* In the blink of an eye, it was transformed until the hand she saw now was simply her own, hanging awkwardly in the air.

"Kerri? Do you agree or not? If you let us handle things, I see no real need to tell O'Connell that I saw you here today, okay?"

"Okay," Kerri answered. She restrained an urge to bolt. "I'd better be getting home."

"Sure," Roberts replied softly. "You try to stay out of trouble from now on."

Kerri walked away on wooden legs. She could feel Dylan's eyes crawling over her as she concentrated on placing one foot in front of the other. *Will he follow me home?* She fought the need to look back. When she had made it to the bottom of the cliff, she scanned the top, expecting to see him standing over her, but he was nowhere in sight.

# CHAPTER 21

**THE DARKNESS WRAPPED** around him like a blanket. He listened to the night chorus of crickets and sat back to wait. *He better not be late.*

He'd been waiting for a while and his eyes had gotten used to the dark. But as he kept watch, he couldn't help but notice how easily ordinary shadows began to take on shapes, almost tricking his mind into thinking someone was there when he knew he was alone.

*No wonder,* he thought, *why so many people are afraid of the dark – jumping at shadows.* He smiled at the idea. *Better to be a shadow, than to be afraid of one.*

He heard the rustle of leaves, followed by a quiet whisper. "Hey, where are you?"

"Here."

The figure approached him, as if born out of the shadows, slowly becoming more visible. "I'm here. Now you want to tell me why?"

"You know why. We've been through this. The little girl is getting in my way. She's poking her nose where it doesn't belong and it's going to stop."

"She doesn't know anything. She – "

"I said that it's going to stop. One way or another, her little game of junior detective is going to end." He could feel the anger boiling up. He clenched his jaw tight, taking a few deep breaths. The still, summer night air invaded his lungs, soothing him. *Anger*, he thought, *would do no good*. "Now, it's your choice. Either you stop her, or I will."

There was no reply to his words, just a quiet retreat that left him, once again, alone, another shadow in the dark night.

# CHAPTER 22

**KERRI LEANED AGAINST** Ann's apartment door that night and checked her watch with a frown. *She's probably working ... but Ann usually takes the early shift.*

Kerri really didn't want to go to the diner to check. Her encounter with Dylan Roberts had left her too worked up. She was afraid that the moment she laid eyes on Ann, she would blurt out everything. *I'd probably walk in and make an ass out of myself, embarrass Ann, maybe even get her fired.*

Kerri groaned, knocking again. *Maybe Ann was napping. She did have to get up at four o'clock in the morning most days.* Kerri put an ear to the door – nothing.

"Where is she?" Kerri asked, impatiently. "I've got to talk to her – now!"

Kerri's mind had been reeling all the way home from the pond. Later in the evening, she had asked her mother to borrow the car under the pretense that she needed to pick up a book she'd been assigned for summer reading. Her mother had raised her eyebrow in a silent accusation that Kerri had ignored, attempting to remain as calm as possible.

The hand she had seen in front of Officer Roberts had most definitely been her father's. The wedding band she had glimpsed was an exact match to her mother's. *What did that mean? Had her father taken Robert's badge? Was that why it was in the box holding his personal things?* Kerri groaned and checked her watch again. Barely five minutes had passed. Kerri picked up her bag, deciding to walk around to the street front. *I'll pop my head in the diner,* Kerri thought. *I'll see if Ann's there. I can do this. I don't have to become the town spaz.*

She was about to lock up her car before she went into the diner, when she heard a car pull up. Kerri was relieved to see Ann in the passenger seat and was about to wave when she saw that it was Seth in the driver's seat.

*Ann was with Seth! Why? After all those things she'd said, why was she out – God knows where – with Seth?*

They looked as if they were chatting comfortably, as though it were a regular occurrence. Kerri slipped into the driver's seat of her mom's car, sinking low into the cushions. All she could think about was Seth's insinuation about Ann. *Seth said that Ann was trying to keep us apart. But look at them! Any idiot can see that there is no "us" to keep apart.* Kerri's cheeks flamed hot. She felt foolish. Their happy smiles seemed to mock her.

Ann climbed out of Seth's Jeep and gave a quick

wave before heading upstairs to her apartment. Kerri tried to dispel her anger, but it burned slow and steady as she watched Seth pull away. *She's my sister,* Kerri told herself, *and Seth is a friend. I need to give them the benefit of the doubt. It might have had nothing to do with me. They could have been talking about anything, right?*

*There really isn't much for them to talk about though,* Kerri thought dejectedly. *Maybe I should leave. Forget talking to Ann. Forget what I just saw.* But she couldn't. She headed back to Ann's apartment, and the door opened abruptly before Kerri had a chance to knock.

"Did I forget something?" Ann's mouth froze momentarily. "Oh, Kerri. It's you. Sorry, I thought you were someone else."

"Apparently," Kerri replied coolly. "Anything wrong?"

"No, I've just been giving advice again," she forced out a laugh. "I should consider a new career path. I might be able to wear better clothes." She gave a cursory tug on her waitress uniform.

Kerri avoided Ann's eyes. "Did you just get off work?" she asked, fixing a smile on her face.

"Yes, and my feet are killing me." Ann sighed and kicked off her clunky white shoes.

*I can't believe it,* Kerri fumed. *Ann has no intention of telling me that she was with Seth! I tell her everything and she is going to keep this from me?* A deep heat spread across Kerri's cheeks, betraying her inner turmoil by burning bright red.

"Hello? Earth to Kerri ... I asked you how you're doing. What's up with you?"

Kerri thought about telling Ann everything that had happened between her and Officer Roberts. She wanted to tell her about their father's hand, how she had seen it reaching out to grab the golden star. Yet now Kerri hesitated. *Could she trust Ann?* She always had before, but now she was unsure. Now Kerri felt as though the ground she walked on was as soft and shifting as the sand at Deacon Pond.

She shrugged. "I just thought I'd see what you were up to."

"Are you sure nothing is wrong? You looked like you wanted to talk."

Ann's face held the promise of sincerity. But as much as she needed to unload, Kerri held back. "Everything is fine. How about you, what have you been up to?"

"Nothing much. I've been working quite a bit, pulling extra shifts." The awkwardness strained between them like a balloon stretched to the limit, threatening to explode.

"Well you need rest then." Kerri inched backward. "Let me get out of your hair."

"I am tired, but you don't have to go. Why don't you come in and we'll hang out for a while?"

Kerri shook her head, her throat tightening. She swallowed hard. "Another time, okay? I'll see you soon."

"Sure, Kerri, I'll see you soon." Ann's voice was faint as if heard from across a distance.

Kerri hurried to the car, wanting to be far away before she gave in to her tears. She took a deep, shuddering breath. She had always counted on Ann. *How will I deal with all of this without her?* She wiped her wet cheeks with the back of her hand. Pulling away from Ann's apartment was like leaving something vital and delicate behind. Her chest was as hollowed out as a shell found on a sandy beach, deserted by the life that had once thrived within.

# CHAPTER 23

**THE RINGING PHONE** caused Kerri to twitch involuntarily. She tried to maintain a calm exterior as she stood among the serious activity inside the police station the next morning. *Yeah, I'm a decent citizen, concerned about answers in the recent death of an unfortunate local man. Only problem is that I'm much more concerned about the not so recent death of my father,* she thought, feeling the momentary burn of shame. *I should leave.* She glanced wistfully at the door, but the cool metal badge in her pocket stopped her. She patted her pocket.

*I deserve an answer to why this was with my father's things.* She took a step toward the desk.

*But did the answer have to come from O'Connell?*

*If he has the answer, then yes.* She announced herself at the desk, hoping for the final time that fate would step in to stop this, that O'Connell would be out or unavailable. "Sheriff O'Connell will be with you shortly, Miss

Langston," replied the desk clerk. "Have a seat."

Kerri obliged, staring at the floor rather than taking the chance of meeting someone's eye. *This is stupid. O'Connell is okay but, let's face it, he probably thinks I'm nuts. Do I want to give him more ammunition against me?* She stood up, taking a step toward the exit.

"Kerri? You wanted to see me?"

She looked up, stretching her eyes until they finally met his. O'Connell was a tall man. She hadn't remembered that. When they'd last met, she'd been too nervous to pay much attention.

"Let's go to my office where we won't be disturbed," he said, motioning down the hall. Kerri trailed behind him, her heart pumping wildly. She tried to breathe slowly, but her chest ached for air. She sat down in one of the lumpy chairs across from O'Connell's metal desk. Kerri wished she had not come. Suddenly, asking questions of this man didn't seem like a good idea at all.

"So," O'Connell said, as he shut the heavy door. "What brings you down here, Kerri? Did you remember additional details that will help with the Travers investigation?"

Kerri swallowed hard. "Not exactly ... "

"Oh?" He nodded slowly. "I see. Then you're here about Seth? I know you two are friends, but I cannot compromise an ongoing investigation because of that."

"It's not about that either. It's about this." She reached into her pocket and fished out the badge. "I want to know what this was doing in my father's personal things."

As O'Connell turned the shiny brass object over in his hand, Kerri held her breath. *He's going to tell me it means nothing. Hell, maybe it does mean nothing.* She wondered again why she had come here. *Because Ann is no longer available.* Her cheeks burned hot with shame and anger. Why couldn't she have just asked Ann what was going on?

"You say this was in your father's things?"

"Yes, and I want to know why."

"There could be several explanations for this, Kerri. After all, Roberts was your father's partner. This could simply have gotten mixed in with your Dad's stuff."

Kerri bit her lower lip, not trusting herself to respond. *Why did I bother? I knew this is what he'd say.* She turned her head away, blinking against the tears in her eyes.

"Listen, Kerri, I know we have had our differences in the past concerning your father's case, and I want you to know that I personally would never have believed that a man such as your father could kill himself."

"He didn't," Kerri answered through clenched teeth.

"I understand your feelings, and contrary to what you might think, I haven't dismissed what you've had to offer in your father's case. I take any information I get and put it to use if I can. Unfortunately, I must have concrete proof. You know that."

Kerri sighed. She knew that he was referring to her visions. "If I had seen something, I wouldn't be here asking about it." She smoothed a hand across her brow.

"God, I don't know why I came here today. I thought I came for answers, but I'm starting to believe there are none. My Dad is gone," she choked out, "and none of this is going to bring him back." Tears streaked down her cheeks, and she buried her face in her hands.

She heard the chair scrape, and O'Connell walked over and placed a firm hand on her back. "Kerri," he said softly, "you're right. None of this will bring him back, but I know he'd be proud of you. He'd be proud that you've never given up on him or on what you believe."

She faced him then. "I think I know that. I think that's what keeps me going."

O'Connell held up the badge. "Let me run a few lab tests, all right? Let's see what turns up?"

"Sure, we'll see what turns up," she agreed. "Thanks – for everything."

O'Connell nodded and offered a small grin. "Hey, it's my job. I'm still the law around here, and if you can't depend on the law, who can you depend on?"

Kerri silently returned the smile, though her heart twisted inside. The answer to that question had died three years ago. Now with every step she took, she felt as unsure as if there were quicksand beneath her feet.

# CHAPTER 24

**KERRI REACHED INTO** her pocket, but her fingers found nothing but lint. *It's been four days*, she thought. *Why haven't I heard anything?*

"I'm so stupid! Who's to say he hasn't thrown that badge in his desk?" She lay down on her bed and gave a muffled groan into her pillow.

Had O'Connell meant what he'd said about running lab tests on the badge? *If he hadn't, then I'm the world's biggest sucker.*

Her fingers clenched into a fist and her hard nails bit into the heel of her hand. *I might as well face it*, she reasoned. *I tried to see if I would feel something from the badge, but I got zilch.*

*But I saw that hand. When I was in the field with Dylan, I definitely got a clear vision of a man's hand.*

It had been a brief flash, easy to dismiss, but she had seen it.

*I would bet my life that was Dad's hand.*

But why had she seen it? What did it mean? She groaned again, flinging her pillow away.

She still hadn't talked to Ann. Kerri had told herself that she had every reason to be angry. *They have been sneaking around behind my back, for God's sake!* Yet she wondered if it was much simpler than all of that. Kerri had always thought of Ann and Seth separately, each fulfilling a need that she had.

"Let's not forget the green-eyed monster called jealousy," she whispered. Despite everything between them, Kerri couldn't deny that she was still drawn to Seth. She wanted Ann and Seth back in their respective places in her life – at her disposal and not predisposed to one another.

She jumped off her bed and stood in front of her dresser. Kerri's reflection taunted her from the mirror. She could not see her face as a whole. Instead, she saw her face in parts – green eyes, a small nose, lips that were chapped by the sun. Nothing hideous reflected back at her, but she could still not see her face collectively. She saw only pieces, broken bits that might not fit together. Who was she, beyond the image that reflected back at her? Did her small nose mean she was cute? Were chapped lips a sign of anything more than too much time in the sun? And her eyes – could they really be called green? From a distance, they looked green. When she leaned forward, until her nose was inches from the mirror, Kerri could see that they weren't really green. She saw a multitude of colors in their depths – black, yellow, blue, brown, all floating together in a sea of green. The colors moved and shifted as if stirred by some invisible force, as if that is what it took to make it look like the color green.

Were her visions the same, a constant blend of different versions of the truth? Why did it feel as though she had all the essential ingredients, but had failed to create anything of value? "I've got to get out of here. Sitting here doing nothing is making me more nuts than people already think I am."

She hopped down the stairs, prepared to grab a water bottle and head out toward the pond. *I'll leave my mother a note – less hassle that way*, she thought as she grabbed a pencil and paper.

"Going somewhere?" Her mother raised a curved eyebrow.

Stiffening, Kerri let out a thin stream of air. "Yeah, I was getting ready to leave you a note."

"Well, as long as you're not going – "

"I know, I know. I can't go near the south part of the pond. You know, eventually it will be opened back up to the public. Then you'll have to let me go there."

Her mother raised an eyebrow again. Her lips twisted as though she had tasted something unpleasant and wanted to spit it out. "I don't know why you'd want to, but I suppose you're right. I can't keep you away from things like that forever."

*Or ever*, thought Kerri.

Her mother cocked her head toward the front

window. "Were you planning on telling me that you were meeting Seth?"

Kerri's heart thudded in her chest. "I didn't know I was." The words came out in a slow whisper that made Kerri feel as if someone else might have said them. She tucked her hair behind her ears in quick, stabbing motions with her fingers.

"He's coming up the driveway. I don't know if I want you hanging out with him, Kerri. It's not a great idea – "

"See you, Mom," she squeaked out, and moved toward the door like a mouse that was pinned under a tom cat's tail that's been given an opportunity to escape.

Kerri's palms were sweaty, and she banged the door open with more force than was necessary. The loud slam that should have denoted her power, only made her cringe. *Fool!*

"What are you doing here?" She didn't look directly at him for longer than a few quick seconds. She wanted to look tough – aloof – but her face burned. She couldn't keep herself from squirming.

Seth's feet pushed stones around on the driveway. "I guess I had to see you. Can I walk with you?" His eyes held a silent plea.

Kerri shoved her hands in her pockets. Her gaze slipped toward the ground. "Yeah, sure." She bit her lip, restraining nervous laughter that threatened to bubble over.

As they walked, the silence between them grew like a cancer. They were in the middle of the woods now. The thick blanket of pine needles beneath their feet was slippery and unsure. Seth held a branch back for Kerri, and their fingers brushed against each other as she passed through. His skin was warm, slightly rough to the touch. Their eyes met and held, and Kerri found it difficult to breathe. In that moment, she believed he saw her as she wanted to be seen, as if she was one of those girls that was so easy to admire. There was power in believing she could be a girl like that.

*It's not you*, she thought. *Quit kidding yourself. He's just holding back the branch so you can walk through.* She turned away, her face burning. "Thanks," she whispered.

"Anytime." He softly clasped her hand. "Kerri?"

Her stomach clutched tight. Her body was taught, expectant. *What if I see something*, she silently asked their joined hands. Fear gripped her. Their hands were still clasped. She felt the sweat on her palm, the moist heat that he returned. Underneath the fear was a tingle of excitement, a secret thrill of knowing that the wait was over. She squeezed his hand a little tighter.

*No! I'm not going to take my hand away because I'm afraid of what might happen. I'm more afraid of nothing ever happening.*

"What's wrong, Seth?"

"Something ... nothing ... everything." He shook his head. "I'm scared."

Her heart drummed. She wondered if he could hear it. She closed the gap between them, touching his face. "You're going to be fine. Your Dad will fight the charges – "

"It's not that." He brushed a stray lock off her face. "I'm sorry about everything I said, about a lot of things."

"Me too," Kerri swallowed hard, setting her chin high. "And if you and Ann like each other, you don't have to hide it from me. I'll be okay about it."

"Ann and me? What are you talking about?"

Kerri couldn't look at him. She wanted to crawl under a rock. *It was hard enough to see it, so do I really have to talk about it?* She took a shaky breath, trying for a normal voice, but her words sounded tight, as if they were being choked out of her. "I saw you two together. What I'm saying is that I'll understand."

"We were talking about you." He shook his head. "Things are screwed up now. I hope they're not so screwed up that we can't ... oh, forget it," he said, and suddenly he was kissing her.

Kerri stiffened, waiting for her inner self to ruin the moment by sending a message filled with negative things. Instead, it was only Seth, moving closer to her. His hands drew her toward his body with a firm grip on the small of her back. His lips were soft and wet. Without realizing, she had wound her arms tightly around him. She stroked the soft hair at the nape of his neck. He dipped in closer, deepening the kiss, his tongue moving lightly against hers. *Wow,* she thought, *we should –*

"We should have done this a long time ago," Seth finished.

She smiled. "It's like you read my mind."

"No, that's your area," he said and kissed her again.

# Chapter 25

**SETH WRAPPED HIS** arm around her as they walked. "Kerri, I need to ask something of you."

"What is it?"

"You have to stay away ... from me, from the field. You have to, Kerri." His hand squeezed desperately, trying to stop her from pulling away. "Promise me you'll stay away."

"I'll stay away, if you tell me why."

Seth hung his head. "I can't tell you right now."

Kerri held herself stiffly away from him. "Can't or won't?"

"It's not a question of me or what I want," he said as he turned forward to face her. "Please, Kerri, I need you to believe me. I need you to do as I ask."

"Well, I need answers! Like why was your father's badge mixed in my father's stuff, huh? And why do I keep seeing ... " She stopped, feeling as vulnerable as a tree growing atop a steep cliff. If she didn't hold tight, she'd risk a deadly fall.

Seth held up their joined hands. "I know," he said, simply. He met her quizzical look with a tight grin.

"You know about the badge?"

"Yes."

"How?" Kerri blurted out before registering Seth's raised eyebrow. "I mean how did you find out? O'Connell promised he'd keep it low-key."

"It doesn't matter, Kerri. All that matters is that you keep away from me and anything that is connected with Mark Travers's death. I can't protect you if you go looking around – "

She ripped her hand away. "The only thing you are protecting is your father! Did he tell you about our nice little chat? He practically threatened me! And you – you're telling me exactly the same things he told me!"

"I only care about you. I don't want anything to happen to you – "

"What about your father? What if he knows more than he's willing to admit about my father's death? Are you sure you are not keeping me away from anything that will incriminate your father?"

Seth lowered his eyes, burying his face. His hands had begun to reach out to her, but they dropped uselessly to his sides. When he looked up, he stole quick glances at her, as if the sight of her burned his eyes. "Is this what it all comes down to?" he asked. "Is this how we're going to leave things?"

Kerri's acid words burned her throat. "I'm sorry. I shouldn't say these things. He's your father and I know you love him. Of all people, I should understand that."

"You're right, I do love him," Seth said quietly. "I suppose that's the hell of it. I love him, but I love you too."

"You love *me*?" Her heart thudded in her chest, and she let out a pent up breath.

"Yes. I have for a long time." He let out a frustrated sigh. "Kerri, I have things I want to tell you, but I can't right now anymore than I can tell you what to do. I know I have no right to ask you to do anything, especially when I can't give you any reasons, but you have to stay away from the murder scene. You don't know how much danger you might get yourself into. I know about your visions. I know you see things, but things you see in your head are one thing. They might be scary, but they can't hurt you ... they're only visions. The person who killed Mark, he's real and he's still out there."

Kerri thought about Mark, how he had touched her, and how his last experiences had transferred to her. She closed her eyes and pictured her father. His kind eyes and gentle manner told her that it didn't matter where the images came from or even why they came. *All that matters now*, Kerri thought, *is that I learn to use my gift and figure out how to control it so I can get to the bottom of all of this.*

"I don't know, Seth. You're asking me to forget about what I see. How can I do that? I'm the one who keeps getting sneak peeks from the dead. I see what they see, and you know what? I'm beginning to think that it's not the dead people I need to worry about, but the actions of the living."

"Kerri, please – "

"Listen, I love you too, but I can't make the promise you want me to."

Seth let go. "Can't or won't?"

"Both," she answered. "I'm sorry, Seth, but this is bigger than me. Something is directing me. Can't you understand? I have to see it through to the end."

His fingertips traced along her jaw. "I was afraid you'd say that." He leaned forward and placed a soft kiss on her cheek. The warmth of his lips lingered even as the sound of his footsteps quickly faded away.

# CHAPTER 26

**AS HER HEAD** sank into her soft pillow the next morning, Kerri's fingertips danced across her lips. The kiss replayed in her mind, soft and sweet. Seth loved her. She relished the words, but she could not focus on his declaration as a girl in love should be entitled to do. The good feelings were shadowed by fear. She could see that Seth was afraid.

It would have been so much easier to promise him that she'd lay low, but she couldn't bring herself to do it.

*For God's sake*, Kerri told herself, *of course he's afraid, there's a killer out there! As long as Mark's killer is free, nobody is safe.*

*We haven't been safe for three years. Dad's killer got away with murder.* The flesh on her arms prickled with goose bumps.

*I can't wait any longer. I have to call O'Connell.*

She was about to rip her door open, when she

stopped cold. *Mom ... where's Mom? I don't want to upset her. I don't want her to hear my conversation and know that I saw O'Connell, not unless I have some real proof to show for it.* She eased the door open and each small squeak from the hinges crashed in her ears. Her mother's bedroom door was shut. She put an ear to the door, her heart pounding, her shallow breaths rasping in her ears. Kerri heard a rustle from within, followed by a sniffling sound. Her mother was crying.

Her heart clenched. She wanted to go to her mother, comfort her, but she could not bring herself to open the door. She stuffed her fists against her mouth, pushing down the urge to cry out. She turned away quickly, lengthening the distance between them before she could change her mind. Her feet swiftly skimmed the staircase.

Quickly, she reached out for the phone, and the mechanical twitches and hollow ringing stilled her emotions. *Pick up, pick up, pick up.*

"O'Connell."

"Did you find anything?"

"Pardon?"

"It's me, Kerri Langston. I have to know. It's been days. Why haven't you – "

"Kerri, calm down. I don't think I need to remind you that these things take – "

"Time? Well yes – it's been three years!" She heard him sigh, and she regretted her harsh words. *I need his help. I may not like that, but that's the way it is.* "I'm sorry," she said softly. "I know you're trying to help me."

"Kerri, as it happens I have some of the reports back on the badge, but not everything. Your father's case is a cold file. It's considered closed around here. It might not seem fair to you, but the Travers case has to be our priority. Understand?"

She ground her teeth to stop herself from screaming "No!" She swallowed hard and took an uneven breath. "You said the reports came back?"

"Yes. The tests aren't complete, but I found three sets of prints. One set belonged to Dylan Roberts of course, since it was his badge. One to your father, and the last set was unidentified."

"Unidentified?" Kerri asked. "It could be anyone? Can't you test it for DNA or something? Can't you find out who it is that way?"

O'Connell spoke carefully. "Yes, but not in this case. Prints like these, they're left from the oil that is secreted from the fingertips. You touch something and *bam*, there's your print. The only way that we could test a print for DNA would be if there were human cells present, like in blood or saliva, something like that. I can tell you that it's possible the third set might belong to a female, but that is only based on the size of the prints. That isn't absolutely conclusive. I'm sorry I can't tell you more at this point."

"If it is a woman, is there any way to find out who she is?"

"We're searching the database, but unless she was a government employee or a criminal, she won't be in our system. We did find trace evidence of blood though."

"Whose blood?"

"I don't know yet. It's probably from your father. We'll cross-check his service records for type when the lab gets back to us with the analysis." He was silent for a moment. "Kerri, we don't know what any of this means. It may take some time before we have any answers."

She nodded, knowing it was useless because he couldn't see her.

"Kerri, are you okay?"

Before she could answer, the line went dead.

# CHAPTER 27

"**WHAT THE HELL** do you think you're doing?"

Kerri spun around. She couldn't move. Her feet were weighed down. The phone receiver slipped from her hand and crashed loudly to the floor. She tried to speak, but her mouth hung open like a rusted hinge. Her mother's eyes were red-rimmed from crying, but they blazed with anger.

"I asked you a question! What are you doing?"

"I – I called Sheriff O'Connell. I needed some answers, and he said he wants to help – "

"Who gave you permission to do that, Kerri? How is digging through the past going to help anyone?" Her voice broke. Her eyes lost their fire. "He's gone, Kerri. Nothing anyone can do will change that. Believe me, if it were in my power to change things, I would."

"Mom," Kerri pleaded. "I know it hurts. I wish I could explain why I have to prove that Dad didn't kill himself. I just have to. Can't you see that it weighs on me? All the time, it's dragging me down." She pressed her fist against her heart. "It's like something is dead inside me, and it won't ever be alive again if I don't find out the truth."

Her mother folded into one of the kitchen chairs. Her body slumped as if she was slowly deflating. She turned her face away from Kerri. "What if the truth is worse?" she asked, hollowly. "Every day since he died, I live with the fact that I failed him. When he needed me the most, I let him down."

"Mom, it isn't your fault. Someone killed Dad, and I'm going to find out who it was."

"You can't kill someone that's already dead." Her face crumpled in pain. "Don't you see? I did it. I killed your father. I may not have pulled the trigger, but I drove him to it!" She buried her face in her hands.

"No! Don't say that!" Kerri rushed forward, kneeling at her mother's feet. "You're not responsible."

"Yes I am."

"What are you saying? Do you know something? Please, you have to tell me. We can talk to the police – "

"No. No more police," her mother said, shaking her head. "That's how this mess started." She grabbed a paper towel and roughly wiped her wet face. "Kerri, I'm ashamed of how I handled things. I behaved so badly." Her lips twisted with self-loathing. "Your father and I – we were having problems."

"Problems?" Kerri asked, slowly. Her body stiffened. The clock on the wall ticked loudly in the momentary silence between them. It was a novelty clock, shaped like a dog. Her father had bought it at a flea market. It had driven everyone nuts because every hour the tail would wag, the eyes would shift from side to side, and it would emit strange electronic barks that didn't sound at all like a real dog. Finally, her father had agreed to flip the switch that silenced the hourly dog noises. Kerri had not heard the clock in years, hadn't noticed it there, still hanging on the wall where her father had put it, quietly marking time.

"Oh Kerri, I don't know how or why it started. He was just so distant. He stopped talking to me." Her eyes welled up with tears. "God, I was so lonely, so weak. I never meant for anything to happen."

Kerri stood up. Her legs throbbed as blood rushed down, stinging like a thousand tiny, sharp needles. "What are you trying to say, Mom? What did you do?" The words ground like glass in her throat.

She twisted the damp paper towel in her hand. Her fingers were taut, gripping it as if it were a lifeline. Her head hung low, accepting defeat with an air of quiet dignity. "We started to meet for coffee. I told myself that it was only natural. He was as concerned as I was." She closed her eyes, let out a sigh, shaking her head slowly. Her hands cupped her face, then slid down dragging the flesh into a momentarily horrid, long mask before releasing it. "Before I knew it, we weren't talking about your father anymore. I knew it was wrong, but your father was becoming so secretive. I thought he didn't love me, that maybe he was having an affair. He told me what I wanted to hear, that your father was on edge, wrapped up in some case. I went because I thought I was helping your father, but now, I know I was only helping myself."

"Are you saying that you cheated on Dad? Who was this guy? How could you do it?"

She held up her hands to ward off the attack. "No. It never went that far, Kerri. I stopped it, before it went that far. I told Dylan that I loved my husband, that I couldn't betray him."

"Dylan? Oh my God! You were meeting *Dylan*?" Kerri covered her mouth with her hand, trapping her words with her shocked expression before they spilled out.

"Kerri, I went to your father and told him everything. I was prepared for him to be angry with me, to hate me, but he told me he understood." Tears streaked down her face. "He stood there looking like I had kicked him in the stomach, and told me he wasn't angry."

"Dad loved you. Of course he'd forgive you, Mom."

"But did he?" her mother asked. "God! I was so stupid, believing him when he said he was fine. I betrayed him! Then I just let him waltz off to work like it was any other day." She shook her head in disgust. "I rushed after him though. I followed him to make things right. But I wish I hadn't gone up there that day – to the hill – because I saw it all."

Kerri grabbed her mother's arm. "Why didn't you tell me? How could you keep something like that from me?"

"Oh Kerri, like a fool, I thought Dylan and your father were fighting over me, but as it turns out, Dylan was trying to stop your father from killing himself. And, in that moment, when I shouted to them to stop, your father was killed."

Kerri sank to the floor. "You saw Dad shoot himself?"

Her mother ran a shaky hand through her hair. "I saw Dylan struggling to pull the gun away. I heard the shot. Can't you see? It's my fault. If I would have just trusted your father and not have run around behind his back, crying on Dylan's shoulder, your father would be alive today. Now I have to live every day with the knowledge that my weakness probably destroyed him! I'm the one who killed him." Her mother sobbed. "It was me."

Kerri wanted to tell her mother not to be foolish, that she was not responsible for what had happened, but the words were caught in her throat. All this time, her mother had not been honest. She had let Kerri struggle alone.

*Mom knew there was more to Dad's story. She knew I felt it, but she just sent me off to Dr. Porter and let him medicate me until I got smart enough not to talk about it anymore. And for what reason? Because Mom didn't want to talk about it, because she felt guilty about what almost happened with Dylan?*

*Maybe that means she is guilty,* Kerri thought. *Maybe there's more than one way to kill someone, and more than one way to lie.*

# CHAPTER 28

**THE SUN WAS** sinking in the sky when Kerri sat down on a jagged rock, ready to admit defeat. The conversation with her mother had left Kerri mentally drained at the same time as it had made her itch to be outside with her feet pounding on the earthen paths. So she had made her mother a cup of hot herbal tea and bolted from the house the minute her mother had fallen into an exhausted sleep. Kerri had hiked up to the abandoned pot field, spending the last hour scouring the ground for clues, before heading toward Mark Travers's abandoned home. The enormous house loomed over her. When she peeked into every dusty window within reach, she saw nothing but cluttered, unused rooms and furniture covered in white sheets like Halloween ghosts. She'd turned the front doorknob, relieved to find it was locked. Above the door, a large mounted fish had stared at her with lifeless eyes.

The dead fish eyes reminded Kerri of her mother's

eyes when she made her confession about Dylan. Her eyes had looked the same – vacant, as if she were staring at nothing in particular, unable to see.

*God*, thought Kerri. *How could my mother have contemplated having an affair, and with Dylan of all people? Dad saw him almost every day. They were partners for Christ's sake. He would have found out.*

"Maybe that's what she wanted," Kerri whispered. "A woman who has a near affair with her husband's best friend probably wants to get caught. She wants to get caught before she's done anything wrong, before she's gone too far, before it's too late."

The more Kerri thought about her mother, the more she pictured the mounted fish above the doorway of the old Victorian house. *They were the same, really*, Kerri thought. On the surface, they were both exposed, vulnerable, but you couldn't see what was underneath, under the skin. The fish had been stuffed to look as though it was still alive, but what about her mother? What lay beneath Lisa Langston's surface, under that part of herself she showed the world? Kerri had thought for so long that her mother had become a zombie, going through the motions of life with no real depth of feeling to show that she was still among the living. Yet after hearing her mother's confession, Kerri wasn't so sure. The fish above the door could never spill its dark secrets, but her mother's confession had shown that there was still life inside her, though it wasn't all that pleasant.

Kerri shifted on the rock, bringing her knees into her

chest. She wrapped her arms around her legs, hugged them to her, and clasped her right hand around her left wrist. She let out a heavy sigh. Somehow, despite her best efforts, she had missed something. The stones she touched had no secrets to spill. The trees silently danced with the wind. No matter how much Kerri felt there was something to be found, she could not find it. No vision, no ghost appeared to point the way. All her life, Kerri had wondered why she saw things, why her? Now when she wanted to be told or shown what to do, nothing or no one came. She was alone.

Yet somehow she did not feel as if she were alone. Her skin tingled, as though an invisible spider walked nimbly up her arm, as though an imaginary hand wrapped its cool fingers around her naked ankle. Kerri shuddered. It was silly, but she found her hands sliding up and down her arms, trying to brush away bad thoughts along with the goose bumps.

She glanced over her shoulder. Why couldn't she shake the feeling that someone was watching her? Every nerve in her body was heightened and on alert.

*Seth was right*, she thought. *I shouldn't be here.* She cast another nervous glance behind her. *I have to get out of here. The only thing I've picked up is a severe case of the creeps.*

She got up, anxious to be moving, to be doing something. When she reached the wooded area that served as a buffer between the house and the field below, she turned for one last look at the old Victorian house.

From her vantage point, the darkening sky cast eerie shadows across the topmost windows. A shifting shape appeared, passing quickly by a darkened window. *Oh my God*, she thought, *is someone in the house?* She blinked hard, but now every shadow was suspicious. Kerri let out a panicked breath.

*If I run, I can make it home before dark. I hope.*

She sprinted through the wooded path, branches whipping in her wake. Soon she was back in the abandoned pot field. She planned to go directly to the south end, ready to scale down the gentle slope back to the trails. Yet she felt herself drawn to the steep ravine in which Mark Travers had met his fateful end.

Peering over the edge, her legs were like jelly and her heart hammered in fear. Mark must have felt like this. She remembered her vision, the moments before his fall when he knew it was coming and there would be no stopping it. Backing away from the edge, Kerri shivered with a sudden chill. *I've got to get away*, she thought. *Something feels very wrong.*

*Run, Kerri.*

She obeyed the voice in her head, not caring whose advice it was, simply ready to follow the order. But the moment she turned around, Kerri realized that it was too late to run. Officer Dylan Roberts stood blocking her path.

# CHAPTER 29

**HE PLUNGED THE** syringe deep into her arm. "Nighty-night," he whispered.

"No," she cried, and jerked her arm away. But the drugs worked quickly. Her heart slowed. She staggered and crumpled to the ground.

He had warned Seth, given him a chance to get his girlfriend under control, but now that the problem had fallen so neatly into his lap, he'd deal with it right here and now. *Really*, he thought, *it's the way it had to be.*

He reached into his bag and uncoiled the thick rope. He grabbed her arms and tied them tightly, before he moved on to her feet. He tugged hard at the rope. *The tighter, the better*, he thought. He grabbed the chunky knot of rope above her wrists and started to drag her. Her head bobbed up and down. Her body bounced against the hard ground. He lifted her over the cluster of stones and the effort made him sweaty. *Heavy*, he thought. *Even for a teenage girl. I should have waited to push the drugs, made her walk at gunpoint.* Even as he thought this, he realized he had enjoyed seeing her fall to the ground. She hadn't been able to say a thing. She hadn't been able to put up a fight. *But eventually she would,* he thought. *When she wakes up, she'll be ready to fight. And I'll be ready for that.*

*She's just a girl,* he thought. *She's just a heavy lump of dead weight. She'll do what she's told, if she knows what's good for her. And if she doesn't? Well, then she'll find out how things really are.* He heaved forward, pulling with more force than necessary, not caring what her body hit along the way. Her legs dragged along the ground, her sneakers filled with dirt. He walked with purpose, his black shoes crunching against the tiny stones in the walkway around the old Victorian house. He reached into his pocket, unclasped his sunglasses and slipped the metal arms over his ears.

*Should he put her with the others?* He needed time to think, time to decide. It wouldn't do to get sloppy now.

*But wasn't it time to teach Seth a lesson about loyalty? Or should he simply rid himself of this nuisance, once and for all?*

He sighed. This was the part of the job that became tedious. He liked making arrangements, setting up safe places to transfer their shipments and, of course, he liked arrival day. He liked looking into their eyes and seeing the naked fear that lingered there, mixed with just the tiniest twinge of hope. Especially when they saw his uniform – they'd get that bright look of hope, an expectation that they were about to be saved from the hellish nightmare they'd woken up in. It would all change soon enough. Their pleas would be wasted on him, just like the tears they would spill on the floor. When he would turn his back to them, they'd quickly realize that the nightmare was just beginning.

*It all gets so damn tedious*, he thought. *Keeping them doped up, listening to their pathetic crying. And the smell – let's not forget how bad they smell after two weeks of laying in the same stinking clothes.*

He looked forward to moving the cargo. He didn't care where they'd go next. He had an idea of where they went. He had heard things – street corners, massage parlors overseas. Girls ending up in dirty trailers, strapped to beds, or holed up in some rich guy's closet – a housekeeper by day, whatever they're told by night. Hell, he'd even heard some ended up as nannies, sold in servitude to some rich family, forced to cook and clean and care for brats all day without pay. He doubted if any of them ever saw home again.

*Even if they had the chance to return to their families, they'd be too ashamed. They would never be accepted back into their homes. What father would take back a daughter who dishonored him in such a way?*

But he didn't care about that. Where they went, what happened to them – it wasn't his concern. What mattered now was taking care of this nosey little girl.

She was his now. He smiled. When he had drugged her, he had stood close enough to see the fear in her eyes.

*She's no different,* he thought, *than any of the girls I move. Trafficking – what a stupid word for it. Traffic was being stalled on the roadways. Traffic was not being able to move. No, compared to that, this business flowed freely.*

*The only difference between this nosey little girl and the girls in my shipment is that she's from around here. She's not some hick from far away, clinging to a stupid dream of going to the city to become a famous actress. She's not a street kid with a drunken father who didn't even care she'd left. Other than that, she could be one of them.*

*She will be one of them.*

# CHAPTER 30

**KERRI GINGERLY CRACKED** open an eye. Her body ached. Her head felt as if it might split in two. *Where am I? What happened?*

*Dylan*, she thought. *Dylan is what happened.*

She strained her eyes, but she couldn't make out anything discernable. The room was dark and shapeless. *No windows in here*, she thought. *And it smells like mud.* Kerri felt so tired. Part of her wanted to drift back into the blackness, to go back to sleep where she could dream this place away.

*You can't do that, Kerri. You don't know where Dylan is, but he'll be back. Count on that.* Shadows moved around her, blackened blobs that had no form. She blinked hard. *Is that a person? Could someone be in here with me?* She heard a scraping sound, a sound that reminded her of a child scooping beach sand into a pail.

"Hello? Is anyone there?"

*It's just a mouse, right?* Kerri shivered. It was damp and cold.

Kerri tried to move, but her arms were pinned behind her. Her feet were tied to the legs of the hard, wooden chair she sat on. She struggled against the ropes, pounding her body against the chair, but it was useless. The harder she struggled, the tighter the knots began to seem.

She collapsed in the chair, a desperate sob escaping from her lips. *Why was this happening? Why hadn't she listened to Seth?*

"Don't fight." The muffled voice came from out of the darkness. "It will be really bad for you if you fight."

*It's not him*, she thought. *It's not Dylan – it's a girl. What was she doing here? What was here exactly?* Then Kerri remembered the vision she had in the field as she held the barrette. A sinking feeling rose within her. Had she seen this girl in her vision, or had she seen herself in the vision?

"Who are you?" Kerri asked.

"Anya."

"Anya, I'm Kerri." She licked her dry lips. "Please, can you tell me what's going on here? Why are you here? And where are we?"

"So many questions – I can't answer so many questions." She sniffled in the darkness.

"Please, Anya, we have to get out of here! You have to tell me where – "

"I don't know where we are," Anya said with a strangled sob. "I don't know anything anymore. The only thing I know is that one day I lived a nice life on my family's farm. Now I'm stuck in a filthy hole in the ground."

In the dark, Anya's words sounded heavy and thick with sleep. Kerri was so tired. It was a struggle to listen. "Anya, how did you get here?"

Anya sighed. "I'm not sure. We traveled for weeks, always at night. We'd get tossed in dirty trucks, freight cars. I screamed, but nobody heard. I cried, but nobody cared." Anya sniffed loudly, trying to stifle the flow of tears. "I miss my family. I miss our little farm." Her voice hardened. "Before this, I complained all the time. I told my parents that I was sick of milking cows; sick of being poor. I was counting the months until I could get of out of there, go to college, and see something of the world besides some crappy little Tastee-Freez on a Saturday night. But now all I want is to hang out with my friends, eating dipped cones, talking about what we'd do when we left town. I want to go back home, back where I know every nook and cranny, back where I am safe and loved."

Anya's voice cracked, but when she began again it sounded soft and husky. "My dad had this broken down car. The thing was up on blocks more than it was on the road. One day, he decided to up and sell it. I told him, 'no one's going to buy this hunk of junk car, no one we know, anyway.'" She let out a sad little laugh. "I was right. One day this guy came around to look at it. I told him to come back later, because my dad was out. The man left and I forgot all about him. I was getting ready to leave for school. I had a new top on, and I couldn't wait for Sammy to see me in it." Anya started to cry. "Sammy's my boyfriend. Well I guess he still is. We were going to meet at our usual spot." She cried harder. "What an idiot I was!"

"What do you mean?" Kerri asked. Her arms pricked with goose bumps. Dread filled her.

"I mean the bastard never wanted to buy my father's car." Anya choked back a wet sob. "He was looking for girls. Stupid girls who walk alone on back roads. The kind of girl who won't think twice when a stranger asks for directions because she's trusting. Yeah, that's the kind of girl he wanted. A stupid girl he could turn into a slave."

"Anya," a voice warned. "That's enough."

"Mari, I'm sorry," Anya sobbed. "I'm sorry. I just want so much ... I want so much to go home."

Kerri, on the verge of tears at Anya's story, sucked in a sharp breath and turned her head in the direction of the new voice. "Who are *you*? God! Who else is here?"

"I'm Mari. There are six of us now, counting you. We lost two."

"Lost?"

"Dead," Mari said flatly. "One girl died before we left the city. They keep us drugged. Pita, she was such a tiny thing. I think she died of an overdose. She just never woke up."

"Oh my God," Kerri whispered.

"Maybe it was for the best. Pita was a runaway. She was the worst kind of runaway – the kind that no one is looking for, the kind that doesn't have a home to go back to. And then there was Olivia. She died when we crossed the state line." Mari softened. "Olivia, she was so beautiful! She was going to be a model. She easily could have been too. She had this long, blonde hair that went down to her waist and big, blue eyes. And she was tall and strong – so strong! She escaped the ropes, had to break a wrist to do it, but she got away. They found Olivia the next morning. She had not gotten far. How could she? We were high up on a mountain road – there was no where she could go but down. She fell to her death."

Unbidden, an image of Mark flashed through Kerri's head. But this girl – this young girl who she did not know, who she would never see, did she have someone to cry for her? Would anyone know how she died? *Mark has me*, Kerri thought. *But who will witness Olivia's death, except those who caused it?*

Mari sighed. "I don't know if it was her injuries that caused her to fall or if she knew there was no other way out, but I know I've envied Olivia. I've been here, stuck like a pig in the mud, and I've envied her. But I've pitied her too."

Kerri's eyes were becoming used to the dark now. Her head seemed less fuzzy, and now she began to be aware of the movements and sounds around her – shallow breathing, scuffles on the floor. Mari scooted closer to Anya, close enough for Kerri to begin to make out a vague outline of her face. *She seems so young, maybe a year or two older than me, but the way she speaks – so tired – it's like she's a hundred years old.*

"Why?" was all Kerri could say.

Mari looked back at her, the whites of her eyes

glowing in the dimness. "Why, you ask? Why did they take us? Or do you want to know what they will do with us?"

"Yes," Kerri said, "and no. I think I can guess what they're planning. I think I know what men like this do to women. " She hung her head, unable to face Mari, as if this were somehow all her fault. As if she could have known that something so dark and terrible lay beneath the surface of her town.

*Maybe I should have seen it*, she thought. *Maybe I should have known.* "Mari? Have they been violent with you, any of you?" As Kerri asked the question, she was almost glad for the dark now to hide her face.

"Only me," said Mari. "And only once. They hit, but anything else," her voice hardened, "anything else is like damaging the merchandise."

"Oh," Kerri felt sick. She wanted to tell Mari she was sorry, but what good would that do? "Is that what you meant, about Olivia? Is that why you envy and pity her at the same time?"

Mari sighed. "Yes. It's over for Olivia. It's just beginning for me. And for the rest of us."

Kerri felt the fear slip back into her chest. She was in this now too. What if Dylan sent her along with the others? What if she disappeared from Westford forever? How long would her mother look for her before she gave up?

*How long before I give up? Before Olivia's fate becomes my own?*

"Soon," Mari said, "he'll be back."

*Soon.*

# CHAPTER 31

**THEY WERE ARGUING**. Kerri could hear their voices, hot and angry, coming from outside. *It's Dylan, definitely him, but is the other voice Bob from the Shop 'N Save?*

Kerri tried to tell herself that she was mistaken, but the more she listened, the more certain she was that the other man speaking to Dylan was Bob. *God, Bob wasn't exactly a prince*, thought Kerri, *but to be involved in this? Kidnapping young women?* Kerri let out a small sound of frustration. She pulled again at the knots around her wrists, the ropes burning against her skin.

"But Dylan – come on, man. What's gotten into you? You're acting all paranoid. You know that the pickup isn't until Friday. That's three days away. We can wait two days, for Christ's sake."

"You tell them that we're not waiting! We do this tonight."

"Dylan, these people, they aren't the kind of guys

that you can order around. They'll kill you as soon as look at you. You know that. You make them a promise, you damn well better deliver."

"In case you've forgotten, Bob, we have a little complication here. How long do you think it'll be before someone misses her?"

"I know, I know, but we'll deal with it, right? I say we can take care of her like we did Mark. Bitch brought it on herself, if you ask me."

"We? Don't you mean me? You should have dealt with Mark when you found out he was stealing, but no, you waited and gave him time to think about ratting us out to the feds. I'm the one who rigged up the trap. I'm the one who served him up like scotch on the rocks. You didn't do shit. You always leave that to me."

"That ain't true! I've stuck my neck out too. Making deliveries through the store, taking care of the girls – "

"Yeah, you've been doing a great job. One of them almost got away. You know what Bob? Get the hell out of here. I've got work to do and I really don't want to have to worry about you screwing up again. Now get lost before I find a reason to haul your ass down to the station. Got it?"

"You're a real bastard," Bob mumbled. "But you probably know that."

Kerri strained to hear more, but there was only silence.

"He'll come down now," Anya whispered. "He's got to feed us and let us go to the bathroom."

"Yes," said Mari. "We go one at a time. We cross the field, go to a house – a very big, very old house."

"Mark's house," Kerri said softly. *So they were close by, but where?*

A new voice broke through Kerri's thoughts. "We are underground."

"Trish's right." Mari said. "That's why it smells like dirt."

"Yes, it smells like earth. Under my body, it feels hard and wet." Trish paused. "I remember being in a place like this, dark and cold. My grandmother's root cellar. My brother – he locked me in – ah, just for a minute! But that minute was horrible. I heard him as he laughed and laughed. Not me. I started to scream. I begged him to let me out. He thought it was funny. He laughed at his joke, until he heard me crying. Then he let me out. I think he was scared too. Maybe just that he'd get in trouble. I don't know, but he let me out then. I was shaking so bad. It had been so dark. I couldn't see a thing, not even my arm in front of me. My brother, he kept saying he was sorry, over and over. He begged me not to tell on him." She let out a strangled laugh. "I never told, but I will always remember the smell and the way I felt in the dark. This place, it is the same."

The door opened and sent a blinding ray of sun into the room. Kerri closed her eyes against the sting of light and turned her head away.

She turned back. The doorway was low, and Dylan had to hunch over. She wanted to yell, to scream, to rake her nails across his face, dig deep gouges in his skin, but she felt paralyzed by her fear. Just then, Kerri saw a glint of steel.

"You first," Dylan said, cutting the top rope on Mari's ankles. He bent low, loosening the rest of the ropes into a puddle on the floor so that Mari could step out of them. She fell toward him and he caught her. He whispered in her ear, "Better not try anything, got it? I won't be as nice as I was before."

He pushed her away, and she stumbled to the floor. "Let's go," he said.

"Stop it!" Kerri screamed. "Can't you see she's hurt?"

Dylan reached out and cuffed Kerri hard upside the head. The blow was hard enough to make the flimsy chair teeter, and Kerri cried out as her eye exploded in pain. "Sit tight, Kerri. No need to be jealous. I'll deal with you soon."

Mari got back to her feet. Kerri knew Mari must be feeling as though she were being stung with a thousand tiny needles as blood coursed down her legs. She took a tentative step before Dylan reached out to give her a hard shove in the small of her back. Mari was propelled outside; the door was shut, and Kerri was left again with the others in utter darkness.

# CHAPTER 32

**KERRI WORKED HARD** now, pulling at the ropes around her wrists. She was bleeding. She could feel it. Her hands were wet and slippery. Each turn of her wrists burned the ropes deeper into her flesh. *But I swear,* she thought, *it feels like my hand is closer to slipping out.*

She could move the rope down, at least a few inches, until it hit the thickest part of her hand. She tried to pull her thumb in as hard as she could to the center of her hand. She tried to make it as small as she could.

*Oh God, oh God, he's coming! You have to hurry. He's coming. You heard what he has planned for you. Hurry!*

But Kerri felt ashamed by her thoughts. How could she think only of herself, when she was surrounded by girls who had been taken from their homes and dragged against their will across the country, as if they were nothing but pieces of meat?

*First things first,* she thought. *I have to get out of these ropes.* She pulled her wrists. She could feel them loosening. The ropes ripped at her skin. Her flesh burned and stung as if hot water had been poured onto it. She heard a pop then, and her hand pulled free from the rope. She bit down on her lip as pain tore through her hand. Her thumb hung limp and useless. For a moment, the pain was too much. She couldn't move. She couldn't breathe. She couldn't think.

*I'm free. Oh my God, I'm free!*

She pulled the other rope off her wrist and began clawing at the knot at her ankles. Her broken thumb screamed in pain, but Kerri did not stop. She pried at the ropes with her working fingers. Her hands throbbed and tingled with newly pumped blood.

"Please, Kerri." Anya pleaded. "Will you untie me too?"

Kerri's heart raced. "I'm almost loose. When I'm done, I'll start on your ropes. We'll make a run for it."

"No," Trish said. "She can't untie you – there's no time. Kerri, listen to me. Run! You must get help – the police, someone. It will never stop if you don't get help."

"What? You want me to leave you here? I can't just leave – "

"You have to!" Trish said. "If you stay, how will you untie us all? Who first? No, there isn't time. You must get out now. He'll be back any minute! You have to run, it's the only way. Get out of here!"

Kerri pulled the last of her bindings away. She stood up, her heart racing and her head so full and confused. *My heart is pulling me in so many directions,* she thought. Kerri thought of her mother and of Ann. She wanted to get back to them. If she didn't run, if she didn't save herself, would Dylan go after them too? Would he go after them anyway?

Kerri thought of the girl named Olivia, the girl who fell – or jumped – to her death when it seemed as though she would not win the fight. *Olivia tried. She went down fighting. And that's what I have to do too.*

"Go," Trish said. "Quickly!"

"Anya, I'm so sorry." Kerri choked out, pushing the wooden door open. The sun hit her. It was so blinding that for a moment she felt as if she might have already died and she was walking through heaven's gate. *Dad, please watch out for me. Watch out for them too.*

She plunged into the white light and started to run.

# Chapter 33

**KERRI HEARD ANYA** scream after her, but she kept running. She ran blindly, her arms pumping. The ground was uneven and her feet thudded hard. Her body jarred clear through to her teeth. She bit her tongue and she could taste her blood, coppery and sweet. She thought she heard desperate animal sobs, but it was her. She ran – ran away from the dungeon, ran away from Anya's pleas.

She pushed through the woods now, breathing hard. Branches tore at her face, like menacing arms trying to hold her back. She could see clearer now; she saw the opening of the abandoned pot field. *I can make it*, she thought.

Kerri looked behind her. Dylan was not there, but she could not shake the feeling that he wasn't far behind. For a moment, she stood mesmerized, waiting for him to pop out of the woods and into the clearing. *Move*, she told herself. *You may have left those girls behind, but you made a promise to help them. You damn well better keep it.*

Kerri's feet began to move again. She headed for the cliff where Mark had fallen. The path she'd scaled up was only a few feet to the left. Her feet crunched over dead plants. She was vaguely aware of her aching thumb, her bloody hands.

*Almost there,* Kerri thought. Then her foot landed on a sharp rock, twisting her ankle and tossing her to the ground. She fell in an ungraceful heap, a frustrated scream escaping her lips. *Get up, get up!*

Kerri had righted herself and was limping painfully forward when Dylan burst through the woods. She hobbled faster, but in her gut she knew he was coming for her, coming too fast. *I've failed. Who will help those girls now? Who will help me?*

She wondered if these were the same thoughts that had run through Olivia's mind, moments before she'd left this world.

"I thought I made myself clear, Kerri," Dylan said as he came upon her, barely out of breath. "Your snooping days are over." His gloved hand slowly removed his sunglasses, folding them carefully before sliding them into the front pocket of his police uniform. Under his gaze, Kerri stood frozen. His blue eyes were cold and clear like ice. "I guess all this snooping around must run in your blood."

Kerri sunk her front teeth into the soft flesh of her bottom lip. The pain was vague and distant.

"Ah, come on now, Kerri, we're old friends, right?

You're not scared of me, are you?" He let out a hard laugh. "I was your dad's partner for years. Hell, you could say his life was in my hands every day. Surely that counts for something."

Kerri bristled at his remarks. "It would count more if he was still alive."

Dylan nodded, unperturbed. "Yeah, I guess you got me there." He crossed his muscular arms across his chest. "But that isn't what we need to talk about is it, Kerri? I guess what we have to chat about is why you had to come up here, snooping around, where you clearly do not belong. More importantly, what am I going to have to do to get you to stop?"

Kerri licked her lips. *Keep him talking.* "I won't tell anyone. If you let me go, I'll keep my mouth shut about everything."

Dylan shook his head, his lips fixed into a sneer. "Yeah, right. I knew it the minute I saw you the first time at Travers's house. I knew you wouldn't be able to keep out of my way. No, you're just like your father, always sticking your nose into things that are none of your business. The way I figure it, you can't help it. Like father, like daughter – two happy peas in a pod. Except your side of the pod had a few upgrades. Not that I believe in all that psychic mumbo-jumbo crap, but I do believe in being careful. And I don't like loose ends."

Kerri took a step backward then froze. She tossed a look over her shoulder. The sharp drop was right behind her. She swayed, feeling dizzy and sick. She thought about

Mark, his dead touch, the terror he had shared with her. *Maybe it was never Mark. Maybe it was always Dad. Maybe he made me see what happened to Mark so I'd find the girls. They're still here and they need my help.*

*Mark,* she thought. *He'd fallen here, but it wasn't only the fall that killed him.* Officer O'Connell had told her that Mark had a bullet hole in his back. The police had also found the remnants of a trigger-loaded booby trap in the field. They had not found the weapon, but Kerri remembered the trip wire in her vision. If Mark had walked into the trap protecting the marijuana field, wouldn't he have been shot in the chest? Kerri supposed that it was possible that Mark had discovered the trap too late and had tried to run, but it was also possible that someone shot him.

*Dylan had said that Mark was going to snitch on them. Was what happened to Mark intended, or was it lucky coincidence for Dylan? Either way,* she thought, *he died right here. I'm standing right where Mark died. Is that a coincidence too?*

"What's the matter Kerri? Do you see a ghost? Careful you don't let one of your boogey-boogey friends scare you and make you take a nasty fall."

"You'd better let me go now. If something happens to me, it's all over. They'll find out," Kerri said with more bravado than she felt.

She made a move to pass him, but Dylan's hand grabbed her arm in an iron grip. "Not so fast." His mouth was so close to her ear that Kerri felt a warm wetness as he spoke.

"Let me go!" she said, pulling hard enough to loosen his grip. Her arm wore a red mark, and Kerri's eyes shifted between her wounded arm and the offending hand that had caused the mark. For a moment, she saw the shadow of a different hand, just as she had the last time she and Dylan had met here. She closed her eyes, allowing her inner mind to travel. Something was coming. She could feel, rather than see, a struggle. As if from a distance, she heard a man's voice.

*Is that Dad?* She strained to hear, going deeper into her secret place, as dark and quiet as a cave. Suddenly, it was flooded with light, as brilliant as a sunny day. The scene that had haunted her for so long replayed. Her father's hand reached out, desperately reaching for the metal badge. The badge twinkled like a nighttime star. Before his hand closed down, Kerri read the engraved name: Roberts. Her father was pleading. *No, don't do this, Dylan.* There was an explosive shot and her eyes snapped open to find Dylan staring right at her. Her throat tightened. Her stomach was filled with hot lava. There was no more doubt. Dylan Roberts killed her father.

*And if I don't do something, he'll kill me too.*

"My mother is expecting me" she said in a small voice. "She's expecting me – "

"To do as you are told and not come out here?" he finished, with the air of a man on an afternoon stroll. "Well, we know how much you've already disappointed her on that score. I don't suppose she'd be too surprised, but I think it's a shame how much pain that woman has had to deal with. But I'd be glad to offer her comfort," he smiled as he mused. "A woman like that? No, that wouldn't be a hardship for me at all."

Kerri's skin crawled at the remark. Then she thought of Anya, walking alone along a country road, in her brand new shirt, a smile on her face as she thought about meeting her boyfriend. *Mom was just as vulnerable. Dylan saw how lonely she was. He sought her out, convinced her to confide in him. And the whole time she never knew that she was spilling her guts to Dad's killer.*

Dylan grabbed her arm roughly, pulling her toward him. "It's a shame though. You and your father have made too much trouble for me to stay around here." He cast a glimpse down the ravine. "I hope you don't mind me being unoriginal, Kerri, but I'm sure a nosey little girl like you would understand if I took care of you the same way I took care of Mark Travers," he sneered. "How does that rhyme go? Humpty Dumpty had a great fall?" He offered a harsh laugh.

Kerri wanted to scream. She wanted to claw at Dylan's jeering face and gouge his eyes out. She wanted to yell that she knew he'd killed her father – that she'd finally seen it – but she knew Dylan would only laugh in her face. *No,* she thought, *just keep him talking!* Her mind screamed. *If you talk about Dad, if you lose it, you're dead. Then he'll never pay for what he's done.* "You" she stammered, "you're responsible for the drugs. You were going to let Seth take the blame for you!"

He shrugged. "Seth brought it on himself. If he'd

followed directions and taken care of Mark from the beginning, he wouldn't be in trouble. I told him – bring my guys over, rough Mark up a little. Let him know what happens to snitches. But no, Seth couldn't stand the idea that someone might get hurt." He shook his head, as though he was simply speaking about his son's poor grades. "Seth can't see what has to be done."

"What ... what has to be done?"

"It's harvest time, darling, time to get paid. We're all networked. Bob at the grocery store, Jim at the bait shop, even that old coot Silas at the antique store. Mark too, before he screwed up and got caught with his hand in the cookie jar. It was perfect, really. See, Mark already had a little homegrown pot stashed away up here. I found it while I was scouting the place out. Old Mark was shaking in his shoes until I explained how he could stay out of trouble and make a little money on the side. Hell darling, the boys and me have got ourselves a system to meet supply and demand." His grin was broad with pride. "It's practically a public service."

"But you're a police officer! You're supposed to protect people. How could you kidnap girls and sell them like objects? How can you go around selling drugs, incriminating your own son – all for some lousy drug money?"

"You think I care about this crappy little pot field? Sure, it's a great side gig, but it's just a cover for the *real* trafficking. If the heat got too close, a drug bust would keep them busy and would give me time to make sure the girls disappear. Not to mention that it would be a good way to shift the blame on someone else if the operation ever got busted. Hell, I don't even handle the pot! I'm smarter than that. I get the others to deal with it. If the police were to get wind of it, they'd never be able to link a thing back to me. Can't say the others would be so lucky – Seth either for that matter." His lips curled in a self-satisfied smile. "Besides, pot's not where the real money is – not that I'd trust those idiots I run pot with to help me with my *other* activities. Those fools aren't capable of handling the ... bigger shipments. You think Jim, the worm king, could handle moving girls? He's a pansy, gets all excited over nightcrawlers. Or Silas? The man has to be seventy years old! He can barely stand to part with the useless junk he calls antiques in his shop. You think he has the balls to keep these girls in line? I don't think so. But Bob, he's a real businessman, a hard ass who's all about profits, usually anyway. Jesus, even Bob has become a real pain in the ass."

"How can you talk like that? Those girls – they're human beings! They have homes – families – that they want to get back to!"

"You think I care? They're nothing to me. They're goddamn cargo – meat I have to move."

"What about your wife?"

"That bitch? She took off the minute she found out how I was making some extra cash. I tried to reason with her, get her to see what a great setup it was. Of course, I kept it simple. I only told her about the ditch weed. Told her it was a no-brainer – that all I had to do for a payout was keep an eye on the field and set up surveillance." Dylan's face was plastered with a look of disgust. "But no, she said it was wrong. She couldn't see that those assholes down at the precinct owed me. She couldn't see I was only collecting what I was due. No, she couldn't see a damn thing my way. She up and left in the middle of the night, didn't even wake up Seth to say good-bye." He let out a bored sigh. "Speaking of good-byes ... "

"They'll catch you." Kerri burst out desperately. "They'll be suspicious, two people falling the same way – it's too much of a coincidence. How long before they suspect you?"

He shrugged. "I won't be here by then. By the time your body is brought to the county morgue, I'll be long gone."

# CHAPTER 34

**KERRI PULLED WITH** all her might, but Dylan effortlessly dragged her closer to the edge. Her feet dug deep grooves in the dusty soil. She thrashed in his grip, the effort causing her to emit animal cries of frustration. She tried to bite down on his hand, but he cuffed her head away as if she were nothing more than a buzzing fly. Angry tears spilled from her eyes.

"I wish you wouldn't take it so personal, Kerri," Dylan said, his face an empty mask. "Really, you brought this all on yourself. If you would have minded your own business, we wouldn't be here."

"No. We wouldn't be here if you hadn't killed my father!" Kerri spat. She couldn't keep it inside any longer. "How could you do that? He was your friend!"

"He was going to blow everything!" Dylan exploded. A corded vein bulged at his temple. "Your father found out I was involved in the drug ring, said he'd have to arrest me. I tried to cut him in on the deal, keep him quiet, but he wouldn't hear it. He tried laying on some crap about how he'd do all he could for me. Do you know what they do to cops in jail?" He slowly shook his head, his lips twisted bitterly. "Jesus, I don't even think he knew about the girls, but he was digging around. Eventually, he'd have found something and I couldn't take that chance. Your father left me no choice."

"You have a choice now," she said bitterly.

"That's where you're wrong, Kerri." He touched his lips briefly to her face. "Don't worry, I'll check on you before I go. Make sure I've ended all your suffering. You see, I do have a heart."

As she fought against Dylan, her mind racing, she thought about her father. When she and Ann were younger, her father had wrestled with them, sharing self-defense tips. *Use his weight*, he'd said. *Use the attacker's weight against him.* Kerri stopped struggling.

She stood still, holding her body taut. The muscles in her legs were screaming. A flurry of birds burst out of an oak tree. They were gone in an instant, a chirping mass of feathers that swooped upward toward the sky. *I'm all alone*, she thought. *I'm all alone on this damn cliff. No, this can't be it*, she thought. *It can't end like this.*

Dylan twisted her roughly around so that she now faced the edge. From behind, Kerri could make out the rhythmic sound of twigs snapping, branches rustling. A flutter of hope swelled within. Someone was coming. "Help!" she cried.

"What the hell?" Dylan uttered.

His grip loosened. *He heard it too*, she thought, glad to know it was not only in her imagination. Dylan released her arms. He reached forward, ready to heave her down the drop with a rough push into the small of her back. He pressed against her. Kerri felt the heft of his body. She could not fight him anymore. He was too strong.

*Use his weight.*

Kerri's body went limp. She ducked down to the ground. Her hands clawed into the dirt. She did everything to cement herself to the cliff, to keep him from taking her down with him. Above her, Dylan lost his balance. He toppled over her. He let out a loud scream. His hands grabbed for purchase, closing uselessly on nothing but thin air. As Kerri lifted her head, their eyes locked. In that moment, she was not sure what was real or imagined, but she knew it was the stuff of nightmares. His icy blue eyes cut through her, holding the promise that they would meet again, before he tumbled out of sight.

# CHAPTER 35

**A STRANGLED CRY** escaped her lips. Like a wounded animal, Kerri did not move. She curled into a ball so tight it was as though she was trying to fold back into herself. Her body shook helplessly.

The hand that dropped on her shoulder caused her to wretch forward and almost lose her balance. "Take it easy now, Kerri. It's all over." Sheriff O'Connell eased her away on unsteady legs.

"He confessed everything," her voice quivered. "He killed my father." Her clenched fists pressed against her pale cheeks. "He tried to kill me."

"He almost succeeded. We saw the struggle."

"He killed my dad," she rasped. "He talked about it like it was nothing."

"Kerri, sit down before you fall down."

"Did you hear me? My father didn't commit suicide. Dylan murdered him!"

"I heard you, Kerri," O'Connell said as he led her to a flat-topped rock. Around them, the woods had come alive. Men were in the bushes below. She sat as still as the rock beneath her as she was gently draped with a grey blanket. *God, his body is down there ...*

"I didn't mean for this to happen," Kerri burst out. "He was going to kill me. I – "

"It's over now, Kerri. It's going to be all right," O'Connell soothed. He kneeled down in the dirt beside her. His black dress socks sagged low on his shins, pooling in his shoes. "Dylan Roberts can't hurt you or your family anymore."

"He kidnapped me. He held me in some kind of hole in the ground – a root cellar, or something. And there are others – oh my God, there are other girls, girls who were stolen from their families." Kerri's stomach lurched and she leaned over, unable to stop herself from vomiting.

"Are you sure about this?" O'Connell asked.

"Yes, oh my God, I'm sure. We were locked up in that place. Tied up in this pitch black hole – please, you have to find them!"

"Jesus," O'Connell muttered. He motioned to a uniformed officer and issued instructions. The officer unhooked his walkie-talkie and began calling for help.

"I came from that way," Kerri said, pointing. "I couldn't see. I just ran and ran." Kerri broke off then, burying her head in her hands. If they didn't find them – Mari, Trish, Anya – she'd never forgive herself.

O'Connell squeezed her shoulder awkwardly. "We'll find them. McCauliff's on it. He'll find them. I guarantee it."

She nodded, swallowing down her panic. She wiped furiously at the tears that streaked her face. "How did you know where I was?"

"Seth. He told us everything – well, everything he knew." O'Connell's hip radio emitted static voices and beeps. "Excuse me a minute."

Although he distanced himself to muffle the conversation, Kerri could see from the expression on his face that he was receiving confirmation that Dylan Roberts was dead. She turned away with a grimace.

"You're a lucky girl, Kerri," Sheriff O'Connell said as he sat back down beside her. "Your quick thinking saved your life. We were too far away ... if you hadn't ducked ... " He shook his head slowly, his eyes drifting over to the drop.

*Luck*, she thought, *could be good or bad. It did not discern between those who needed it and those who did not. It was an intangible force that landed purely at random. I'm sitting on this rock because I got lucky. But then again, I'm sitting on this rock because I'm unlucky enough to see dead people and to follow them when they need me.*

"Kerri, I wish you hadn't come out here, but this is not your fault. Seth – "

"Seth. Does he know ... about his father?"

"Seth has been working with us for some time – his mother, too." O'Connell held up a hand to stop Kerri from interrupting. "I couldn't tell you before. There was too much at risk."

"All this time?" Kerri asked. She raised a shaky hand to her temple. "All this time you let me think Seth might be a suspect?"

"I'm sorry, Kerri," O'Connell said. "But it's true. Seth was never a suspect."

"What about the blood test, the one Dylan said Seth failed?"

O'Connell raised his eyebrows. "Dylan made sure Seth failed. He doctored the record." He let out a heavy breath. "You know, when Seth and Cindy first came to me, I didn't want to believe it. Roberts has been on the force a long time. He had a clean record. The allegations they made against him just didn't seem possible. But Seth told me that his father wouldn't think twice about doing whatever he had to do, even if it meant incriminating his own son. I guess Seth knew the man better than I did, maybe even better than his wife did."

Kerri was stunned. "Seth ... how could he keep quiet about all of this?"

"He had to. His life and his mom's life, they both depended on it. You see, they had proof that Roberts had access to large amounts of cash, but they had no way to link him to the drugs because Roberts was careful. He made sure that he never handled the distribution. Cindy and Seth didn't even know how much money Roberts had or where it all came from."

"What about the badge?"

"Forensic testing has changed since your father was killed, Kerri. We picked up blood splatter – your father's blood – on Roberts's old badge. While that alone was probably not enough to convict Roberts, it brought in new evidence, which allowed us to reopen the case."

"What about the third set of prints?"

"They belong to your mother." O'Connell shifted uncomfortably.

"What? I found the badge in Dad's old police things. I didn't think she ever looked inside that box."

"Kerri, isn't it possible that your mother had no choice, that in order to move ahead, she had to face the past? Everyone grieves differently," he said. Kerri thought O'Connell sounded like a man who knew about grief.

Kerri thought of her mother's confession, about the intimacy she'd shared with Dylan. "She thought it was her fault," Kerri said. "My Dad, I mean. She thought he'd killed himself because ... because of something she'd done."

"That's pretty common in cases of suicide. Now we know differently. Now she can stop beating herself up." O'Connell sighed. "It's unfortunate that your father didn't do a formal investigation. I guess I can see why he didn't. He probably didn't want to believe Dylan had gone bad anymore than anyone else wanted to think. I can't help thinking, though, that if he'd brought his suspicions about Dylan to his superiors, things might have turned out differently."

"All this time ... God! Do you have any idea how hard it has been to live with this? To be told your father had killed himself but to know with all your heart that he didn't?"

"I know you've suffered," he said quietly. "You're not the only one. We've had Cindy Roberts in a safe house for six months. It has killed her to be away from her son, fearing for his safety. The night we placed her in protective custody, she begged Seth to come with her, but he refused. He said he'd gotten in deep with his father, and he didn't want to live that life anymore. He said it was time to change things. So Seth agreed to play along, make deliveries for his dad and help us keep tabs on Dylan while we built our case against him. It's been really hard on Seth. He remembers a different man, a man who tossed a baseball with him, who taught him to ride a bike. A son doesn't forget those things." O'Connell's voice lowered to a husky whisper. "Seth is a brave young man, no doubt about it. His involvement has put him in danger. He almost risked the whole operation when he spoke to your sister."

Kerri hung her head, remembering her petty jealousy. "Seth must have known Dylan met me in the woods, threatened me. He knew what his father was capable of."

"More than any of us did," O'Connell agreed. Kerri saw Seth emerge into the clearing. "I'll need a statement, of course, but I think I had better speak to Seth right now."

Kerri murmured her thanks, watching O'Connell and Seth meet in the clearing. Recognition painted Seth's face with grief. In Seth's eyes, Kerri found an ache that mirrored her own pain. *I caused this,* she thought. *I'm alive because I killed his father! How can he ever forgive that?*

She turned away, burying her face inside her palms. *How can I forgive myself?*

# CHAPTER 36

**THE CEMETERY WAS** large, but Kerri knew precisely where to go. A large oak tree provided shade on one side, while the Virgin Mary watched over the other. Mary beckoned with her stony, marble arms. Kerri remembered her fear of graveyards, so silly and girlish now. She stared at the hard, chiseled stone. Her eyes traced the hands folded in prayer, the letters that spelled her father's name: John Langston.

Since her father's case had officially been marked and closed as a homicide two months earlier, Kerri had not had one episode reliving his death. In a weird way, Kerri almost missed the visions. They had not been pleasant, but they had briefly connected her to her father. It was time, though, for her father to find peace. *I guess,* she thought, *it's like having a huge, hairy wart cut off your face after you've kind of gotten used to seeing it.*

She bent down and placed a single red rose on the

ground next to the stone. Her mother and her sister both took their places on either side of her. Ann slipped her arm around Kerri, giving her a gentle squeeze.

"I feel like I could come here every day for the rest of my life and it still wouldn't seem real," her mother said, as she dabbed at her eyes with a tissue.

"He forgave you, Mom," Kerri said, putting her arm around her mother.

"Maybe, but I'm not sure I can forgive myself."

Ann moved closer. "Time," she said quietly. "Time is what we all need."

In the two months since Dylan Roberts was put to rest, the Westford police had made several drug-related arrests, including the arrest of Kerri's old boss, Bob, from the Shop 'N Save. Bob had used the store's delivery service to distribute drugs throughout the town. Every driver at the Shop 'N Save had taken a voluntary drug test – Seth included – and they all passed. By then, it seemed a mere formality, since the press had already reported that among Dylan's crimes was the falsified test that cast suspicion on his own son.

The local paper interviewed all the employees, who pled innocent to any knowledge of drug trafficking. The official story stated that if the drivers were guilty of running drugs, no driver was ever aware they were delivering anything besides groceries. When the police searched Bob's apartment and seized several pounds of marijuana, Bob began to give up the names of his associates, hoping for a shorter jail sentence.

Bob had tried to deny his involvement in the girl trafficking scheme, but his protests were quickly disputed by the testimony of the girls Kerri had met in the dilapidated old root cellar. The words of Mari, Trish, and Anya had stood out the strongest. They had all demonstrated fearlessness in the court room. Not only had they been able to positively identify Bob, shutting down the operation for good, but their stories had found favor with the media and the public. Local groups set out to provide them with counseling and started initiatives to help prevent other girls from meeting a similar fate. Mari and Trish joined the Angel Coalition, which helped girls who had been abducted and rescued start their lives over.

Anya had since returned home to her family. Kerri had gotten a letter from her. There was something about Anya's words that made Kerri keep opening the letter and rereading it. "Every day that passes," Anya wrote, "I take one step closer to being normal again. I still have nightmares. I wake up in the middle of the night, and I think that I'm back there, in that cellar. I wake up screaming, 'Don't leave me!' That's when I remember that you didn't leave me, not really. You saved me. You saved all of us."

Kerri had written back to her. She had told Anya that it hadn't been her saving them. They had saved each other, but somehow that didn't seem quite right. The decision to run, to burst out of the cellar and into the blinding sunlight, had felt, to Kerri, the same as following one of her visions. There could be no assurances, no way to know if she was headed in the right direction. Running from the cellar that day had required a sense of faith. Kerri knew instinctively that learning to trust her visions would be the same.

By the time a fine sprinkling of grass covered his grave, Mark Travers's death was ruled a homicide. Witness testimony had suggested that, heavily in debt and fearing bank foreclosure on his home, Mark had made a hasty deal with Dylan. The temptation for easy cash proved too hard to resist though, and Mark began to sell small bits of the crop. Dylan had threatened Mark, and Mark had pushed back, threatening to expose their trafficking activities to the police.

Although the physical evidence in the case would not be enough to prove Dylan Roberts had killed Mark, Kerri's testimony had ultimately found him responsible for the crime. Kerri had asked O'Connell whether he thought that Mark Travers would have survived if Dylan had not pushed him down into the ravine. "Left on his own," O'Connell had said, "he might have bled out before he could get medical attention. There is just no way to know, Kerri. Why do you ask?"

"Because," she'd replied, "sometimes I still hear him ask me for help."

Kerri knew O'Connell was right. It was time to let it go. *Dylan is dead*, Kerri thought, *so is Mark. There is no point in pondering whether Dylan killed Mark or if greed walked him into the gun-triggered trap. Either way, both had paid for what they'd done with their lives.*

Kerri stepped away from her family to stand before

Dylan's grave. Someone had placed a solitary planter boasting an array of fall flowers. She knelt down to touch Dylan's cold stone, her body stiff, her hand trembling. Silent tears slipped down, which she quickly wiped away. Her insides were too hollowed out to offer anything more. She felt like a carcass that was stripped bare. She closed her eyes and allowed her fingers to move across the coarse surface. For now, the dead were at rest. The only struggle Kerri felt came from within. She studied her mother's pale face.

"Mom?"

"Yes?"

Kerri didn't know how to say what she was feeling. They'd been over her father's death so many times. They had cried. They had spent long afternoons dreaming about what their life would have been like if John Langston had not been killed. Kerri knew her mother was sorry. She had apologized for her treacherous alliance with Dylan and for the way she had shut out her daughters. Yet Kerri couldn't help but feel as though her mother had said the same things so often that the words had begun to lose their meaning.

*How do I tell her that even though I understand, there are times I still feel angry? Not about Dad, but about me. There's this huge part of me that she's denied all this time. How do I say to her that because she didn't believe in me, couldn't accept my visions, that I learned not to believe in myself?*

Kerri knew she couldn't say that. Her mother had said she was sorry. She had admitted to being wrong.

"Mom," Kerri said thoughtfully. "How do people walk through life every day when they feel so weighed down? Do we ever drop our burden? Get someone else to carry it? How do *you* do it?"

Her mother offered a bittersweet smile. "We all carry our burdens, Kerri. There's no dropping them, ever."

"Way to be optimistic, Mom," Ann scoffed.

"I'm sorry, Ann, but in my life I've found that you can't drop off your baggage just because you're tired of hauling it around." She touched Kerri's cheek. "Honey, all I can tell you is that you learn to let go, a little at a time, until what you have left doesn't seem as heavy anymore." She smiled again, but the gesture did not change the sadness in her eyes.

As they got in the car and left the cemetery, Ann nudged her, saying "I ran into Seth yesterday. He came into the diner with his mom."

Seth's mother had returned to town for Dylan's funeral. The Roberts' home was promptly listed with a realtor, and Cindy and Seth Roberts were now settled in a modest home a few blocks away from the one they had shared with Dylan.

Kerri had not been able to go to the funeral. Facing Seth made her insides twist into knots. She saw Dylan's face over and over in her nightmares. It had been bad enough for her to agree to see Dr. Porter, who had reminded her of what she had already known – that she had no hope to seek Seth's forgiveness if she could not forgive herself. "It takes time, Kerri," Dr. Porter had said.

"Well, I've got that," she had replied.

Ann touched Kerri's arm, returning her to the present. "Kerri, Seth's doing okay."

"Yes, not bad considering his friend murdered his father." Her throat squeezed tight.

"It was self-defense!" Ann threw her hands up, frustrated. "Everyone knows that but you." She touched Kerri's arm. "Anyway, Seth said he wanted to talk to you."

There was a glint in her eye that made Kerri's heart race. "Ann, what did you do?"

"Nothing, except tell him he's welcome anytime."

"Kerri," her mother interjected, "I think what Ann is trying to say is that you don't want to put off facing things for too long. I ought to know." She grimaced as they pulled into their driveway. "Oh girls, I think I'm going to throw up. Do you think I should cancel tonight?"

"No!" Kerri and Ann said in unison and smiled. Her mother and Sheriff O'Connell – Jim – had agreed to meet for coffee that night. The sheriff and Lisa Langston had met often while the final details of John Langston's case were handled, but this would be the first time the pair would meet socially. Her mother had already allowed her nerves to break one date already.

"Are you sure?" She held her stomach, her face contorted in a grimace. "Oh God, I hope this is just nerves." She ran past them into the house. Ann and Kerri smiled.

"On that note, I've got to go. Call me later with details," Ann said.

"Details?"

"Yes, details. Hi, Seth. See you two later."

Kerri turned around, shifting awkwardly while Ann and Seth exchanged greetings. Her mouth formed a soundless "Hello." She cleared her throat and tried again. All that came forth was a barely audible whisper that no one noticed.

She rubbed her sweaty palms together. Her heart beat furiously. She wanted someone to acknowledge her presence. She wanted the ground to swallow her whole. Ann was talking, but Kerri could hear nothing she said. As Ann started to turn away, Kerri felt her stomach clutch tighter. She didn't want Ann to leave.

*I'm not ready!*

Maybe she would never feel ready. She felt Seth shift closer to her as he waved Ann away. His proximity made her body tingle. When he touched her arm, her flesh jumped as if it were electrified.

"Do you want to take a walk?"

She nodded her assent, swallowing hard. She took a deep breath. "Sure," she whispered. Immediately, she wished she could make some excuse not to go. She felt trapped, boxed in like an animal.

*I feel like a guilty criminal*, she thought, *which I am, in a way, guilty of murder. They might call it self-defense, but I still killed a man.*

Shame burned hot on her cheeks. She did not dare look Seth in the eye. She feared his eyes might pierce through her; that they would be his father's eyes and they would brand her forever. She chanced a quick peek at his face, before looking back down at the ground. A fluttery, irrational thought flooded through her. *What if Seth wanted revenge? What if he felt so wronged, so cheated, that he didn't care who he hurt? What if he was like his father?* Her heart went cold. *No, Seth could never be like that.*

But the thought would not leave her, even when Seth began to speak softly. "Where do you want to go?"

They went to Deacon Pond, of course. They filled the fire pit and sat on the beach. The fire started slowly, filling the air with smoke, but grew strong and steady. As Kerri watched the fire build, her own turmoil grew with it. Her throat burned from the acrid air she inhaled, and the smoke made her nose sting as if she were going to sneeze. She blinked to clear her watery eyes, waving a hand to clear the smoke away. She felt like a dry, crackling log in a hot fire, ready to pop under the heat and silence.

She snapped, spitting out, "I'm sorry, Seth." Her voice cracked and real tears sprang from her eyes. Her throat burned. "I don't know what else to say. I'd understand if you hated me ... "

He grabbed her arm. "I don't hate you, Kerri. My father's actions came close to destroying everything." He broke off, clearing his throat. "My father sacrificed our family for money and did such horrible things. He killed your father and he tried to kill you. He kidnapped helpless girls and sold them like slaves." He shook his head. His face wore a sour look, as if he'd just tasted something bitter and unpleasant. "No, I'd understand if you couldn't look at me without seeing my dad." He sighed, turning away. "I don't know. It's hard, because sometimes I feel nothing but hate for him, and other days I remember the person he used to be." A smile haunted Seth's face. "Remember the tree house he built for us?" he said softly. "We were eight, I think. All I said was that I wished I had a tree house and my dad spent weeks drawing up plans, like I was going to live there or something."

"Yeah, I remember. It had a trap door. When you were mad at me, you'd sit on it so I couldn't get in." Tears slipped down her face. She wiped them away, her tongue licking her lips and tasting their salty wetness. "That's the person I try not to remember," she whispered. "Because when I remember who your father used to be, that's when it hits me how much I've taken away. He was still your father. I know what it's like to live without a father."

Seth looked at her, surprised. "How can you think like that? You didn't take my father away, Kerri. He checked out of my life a long time ago. He did it to himself."

"I know," she inserted firmly. The lump in her throat grew. She tried to swallow it down. "I'm just not ready to forgive myself yet." Kerri reached for Seth's hand. "It's going to take time." Little trails of warmth blazed up her skin as Seth's fingers lightly moved across her hand. The tightness in her shoulders began to relax. She took a deep breath and blew it out, emptying her lungs to ease the tension.

Dylan's ice blue eyes flashed briefly before her, giving her an instant jolt, before melting back into Seth's warm, brown eyes. *Yes,* she thought, as she rested her head on his shoulder, *we do need time. We both do. We need time to figure out what will be between us, what kind of relationship we have.* No more hiding, thought Kerri. *Not from each other and not from myself.*

Kerri didn't know if she'd ever be a "normal" girl, but she couldn't worry about that anymore. She couldn't make any more excuses. She was a girl who had a gift. Not wanting it, or pretending it didn't exist, had not helped.

*From now on, I'm not going to crawl up inside myself every time I have a vision. I'm not going to run from what's inside my head any more than I'm going to run from Seth. I'm going to figure out what's there. Maybe how I treat my relationship with Seth isn't all that different from how I treat what I've got going on with the dead. I've been afraid all this time of what they want from me, of getting hurt, but maybe I don't need to be. I guess a girl can learn to trust.*

She and Seth talked long into the night. For the first time in her life, Kerri was going to break her curfew. For the first time, she would be the last one to leave Deacon Pond.

Her father, she knew, would understand.

# Don't miss these great teen reads!
# On Shelves Now!

written by
Kimberly Joy Peters

*Painting Caitlyn*

## Painting Caitlyn
### by Kimberly Joy Peters
**ISBN: 978-1-897073-40-7**

Caitlyn's in her senior year of high school, and it's turning into the worst year of her life. She feels ignored by her mother and step-father who are obsessed with having a new baby, her best friend is always blowing her off for a boyfriend – even art class, the one thing that usually lifts her spirits, has become a struggle. Enter Tyler – older, gorgeous, and totally into Caitlyn. He makes her feel needed and special, and whenever she's around him, her problems seem to disappear. But just as things get serious, Caitlyn discovers Tyler's jealous side. Once she realizes her "perfect" boyfriend is as controlling as he is caring, she is faced with a choice: she can either let this relationship define her, or find the courage to break away.

# Fighting the Current
## by Heather Waldorf
### Hardcover ISBN: 978-1-894222-93-8
### Paperback ISBN: 978-1-894222-92-1

Theresa "Tee" Stanford figures her life is smooth sailing. But everything changes when a drunk driver hits her father, leaving him mentally disabled. With her last year of high school looming large and a friendship teetering on the brink of romance, Tee finds she can no longer rely on her old plans for the future.

"The characters are believably imperfect, and they work through their troubles in realistic ways." – *School Library Journal*

"You are drawn in ... from the very first page ... This is a very intense, very real book." – *Independently Reviewed*

"A meaty read, **Fighting the Current** will leave thoughtful readers ... asking 'Who am I?' " – *CM: Canadian Review of Materials*

**Selected, International Reading Association Young Adults' Choices (2006)**

**Shortlisted, Stellar Book Award (BC Teen Readers' Choice Awards, 2006-2007)**

**Winner, USA Book News "Best Books Awards", Young Adult Fiction Category (2005)**

**Selected, Children's Book Committee at Bank Street College, Teen Booklist**

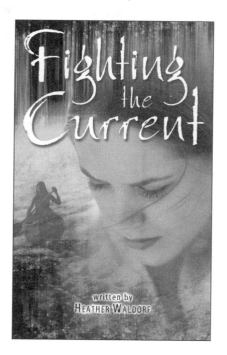

www.lobsterpress.com